FOLK BALLADS OF MITHILA

(STORIES OF FOLK HEROES AND HEROINES LIKE SALHES, LORIK, BIHULA AND OTHERS)

YOGENDRA PATHAK VIYOGI

Contents

Preface

I have great pleasure in presenting the third title "Folk Ballads of Mithila" along with the already published two titles "Folktales of Mithila" and "Gonu Jha of Mithila (Tales of wit and humour)". All three form part of "Mithila's Cultural Heritage".

Mithila, the birthplace of Sita, is well known from Vedic times for her learning, scholarship and spirituality. It is also rich in the traditions of rural culture with its folktales, folk art, folk dance, folk songs, ballads, paintings etc., making a vibrant social life in Mithila. It is necessary to have a good compilation of folk culture and tradition to be passed on to the future generation.

Folk Ballads are essentially long songs describing the heroics of common people. Ballads are different from the poetic creations of learned people. Scholars have called them non-Vedic, rendered by people in the lower strata of society, who are illiterate but have creative power nonetheless. The folk heroes described in the ballads are mostly from lower castes, like Salhes (Dusadh), Lorik (milkmen), Dayal Singh (fishermen) and the like. These heroes/heroines are worshipped mainly by the people of those castes but a few like Salhes have gained wide acceptance within the society and people of other castes also worship and revere them.

The language of the ballads is simple, colloquial and not constrained by the rules of prosody. Still, they are very sweet to the listeners and convey the contents with clarity. For a connoisseur who can read Maithili, I have included a few lines of the original lyrics with English meaning within a box to appreciate the simplistic charm of the composition.

The ballads are sung by artists accompanied by music rendered by local instruments, mainly the Mridangam family of percussion instruments, metal instruments like sistrum and also clapping of hands.

The ballads do not have uniformity; there is no written version like a book; these have been passed from one generation to the next through oral traditions only. They vary considerably depending on the region and the singer. However, the central theme remains more or less unaltered. The story told in the present compilation gives the reader an idea of the society in which the folk heroes and heroines lived in those times and also what made them so important in the eyes of the society that the tales live even today some thousand to fifteen hundred years later.

Scholars who have done extensive fieldwork state that there are altogether 72 stories about various folk heroes and heroines floating around Mithila, comprising both the Indian and Nepali Terai regions.

A large number of scholars have done extensive work in compiling and categorizing the various folk songs and ballads. These works are mostly in Maithili and Hindi. Goerge Grierson called them 'popular songs' and compiled the ballads (with English translation) related to Salhes and Deena-Bhadari.

In the present compilation, I have collected eleven stories. I have benefitted greatly from the works of Prafulla Kumar Singh 'Maun', Vishweshwar Mishra, Yoganand Jha and Braj Kishor Varma 'Manipadma', all being in Maithili.

A very brief introduction to Mithila and its culture has been included which provides background material to help appreciate the subject matter of the tales. I hope the reader will enjoy the tales and appreciate the culture of Mithila. An explanation of some customs and rituals prevalent in society in the olden days is also provided in the Appendix for the benefit of the readers.

Yogendra Pathak Viyogi

Kolkata, July 10, 2024

I
Raja Salhes

[Salhes is a distorted word for the original Sailesh, which means the mountain king. Salhes is the only folk icon which is worshipped even today by almost every section of rural Mithila, irrespective of caste or creed, both in Nepal and India. Wearing a little tilted turban and riding an elephant with a shining tusk, Raja Salhes's clay idol is accompanied by his nephew (sister's son) burglar king Karikanha as a mahout. By his side, his younger brother and minister Motiram is seated on a horse. On another side is an idol of a beautiful woman, Anang Kusma (also known as Kusma Malin) with a flower basket in one hand and a lotus garland in another. A little aside on both sides one finds the tiger 'Thanka' and the bear 'Banka'. This a typical scene adoring the worship place (known as Gahwar or Sthan or simply Than) of Raja Salhes in most villages. The idols may vary in detail in different parts of Mithila. In Mahisautha village of Siraha district of Nepal, which is part of Nepalese Mithila and supposedly the birthplace of Salhes, there is a Salhes temple. Mahisautha Garh, or Fort Mahisautha, was the capital of Raja Salhes. This place is a big tourist attraction in Nepal and a big fair is held every year during the Nepalese new year. Salhes is revered because of his ever willingness to help people in distress; the so-called 'gohari' session being his daily routine where he would listen to anyone who came with any type of distress call.

The 'Malin' sisters, Hiriya, Jiriya, Dauna and Kusma, daughters of King Maheswar Bhandari of Taregna, are in love with Salhes, knowing fully well that Salhes is married to the princess of Virat Nagar. Their love however is very refined and platonic, and none of them desires a physical relationship with Salhes. The sisters are the followers of the 'Malin' sect, famous for Tantric teachings and practices. They are known for their intelligence, beauty, compassion and knowledge of the forests and mountains including the rare herbs and medicinal plants. For this reason, the sisters were often referred to as Vandevis, the Goddesses of the forest.

Although it is very difficult to ascertain the exact period during which the events mentioned in Salhes folklore occurred, experts believe the period to be around the 5th to 6th Century AD when the northern part of Nepal was under constant threat from the invading Kirat and several other Tibetan and Chinese tribes.

The ballads have a significant variation in the narration of the story, depending on the region and the singer, but the central theme of Salhes's 'gohari' and his platonic love affair with Kusma Malin is common to all. Recently a full-length film has also been made depicting the story of Raja Salhes.]

Jayvardhan Salhes was born to a saintly father and a cursed fairy from Heaven, Mandodari, in the Dusadh caste (a low caste in the social hierarchy in India) in Mahisautha village in modern-day Nepal. He had an elder sister, Vansapti. His younger brothers, Moti Ram and Budheswar were also brave. Vansapti was a brave lady who had mastered the art of taming ferocious animals. She was also well-versed in Tantric practices. She was married to the king of Bagh Garh and had a son, Karikanha, who was known to be a proficient burglar, fondly called the Burglar King.

Salhes got married to Satyavati, the princess of Virat Nagar at an early age as per the prevalent social custom. His wife lived with her father as she was young and not of age to live with her husband.

Salhes was as brave as handsome and endowed with compassion which no one around possessed in that measure. He never resorted to any retribution or vindictiveness. Rather he would meet his archenemies also with love and compassion and win over their hatred. He was a devotee of Lord Shiva and Mother Goddess Durga and infallibly he would worship them daily in the morning before commencing his *gohari* session. As a king, he was very empathetic towards the common man, not only within his kingdom but also outside. He always tried to protect the regions in Mithila and bordering Nepal from the northern aggression of Kirat and other Tibetan tribes.

राम राम राम मलिनिया बोलइए
जाहि दिन अकिल बुदधि मोरंग मे भेलै
ओही दिन वरत हम केलियै
सलहेस छोड़ि दोसर बर नै हम करबै
ओही सलहेस पर अँचरा हम बन्हलौं
जीव-जन्तु अँचरा मे फड़ि गेल
जल मकड़ा आइ सेहो बिआइ गेल
तैयो ने डिंगराक दर्शन भेलै

The Malin says "Ram, Ram, Ram"
The day I attained some wit in Morang
That very day I took an oath
I shall never marry anyone other than Salhes
I had tied an Anchara as proof of that oath
Worms have grown in that Anchara by now
They have laid eggs also there
But I could not meet that fellow yet

During one of the *gohari* sessions, a messenger from King Maheswar Bhandari of Taregna came to inform Salhes about the impending attack from the Kirat army. The attacker aimed to kidnap the youngest daughter of the king, Kusma Malin. It was known to the Kirat king that the Malin sisters were devoted to Sahles and had taken a vow very early in their lives not to have any other man in their lives. As proof of this, they had each tied an Anchara. They had waited very long but were singularly unlucky not to have ever met Salhes. (See Box for the original narration in Maithili).

To protect themselves from the attacking enemy; the Malin sisters had left their palace and taken shelter in the mountains at a place called Yogini Caves. This place was secluded and also naturally protected. Salhes got the message about the attack and he sent his own Mahisautha Garh army under the command of Anhar Math and the Bagh Garh army under the command of his nephew Karikanha. The two armies surrounded Taregna and repelled the attacking Kirats without much loss on their side.

When the Mahisautha army was fighting the Kirats, Salhes went to the mountains for a ride and came to the Yogini Cave by smelling the uncharacteristic and heavenly fragrance. He was received by the Malin sisters and he spent a few days there. He learnt much about the qualities of the young beauties, in particular that of the youngest, Kusma. The sisters were also impressed with the benevolence of Salhes.

On another day in the *gohari* session, Salhes was approached by an old man who complained about a man-eater tiger. The tiger had killed his three sons. He had killed many others in several villages and spread a reign of terror throughout the locality. The tiger was always accompanied by a dwarf ghost. Salhes was surprised that such an incident took place for so long and he was not informed. Nevertheless, he assured the old man that his problems would be solved.

The next in line during that session was a person white with fear. He could barely speak. After getting full assurance from Raja Jayvardhan Salhes, he began narrating the woes of the people of his village and surrounding area. They had been threatened by a demon in a woman's shape, who carried with her an army of tigers, bears and wolves. The demon used to kill both humans and cattle and feed her pet tigers and wolves. No one dared stand against her. Raja Salhes again assured the person that this problem also would be dealt with.

Finally came a deposed prince disguised as an ordinary soldier. He narrated the tale of the kingdom of Samdagarh having been taken over by a smuggler with the help of some enemy armies. The smuggler was now catching young women and sending them to Kashi's prostitution market. Salhes recognized the soldier as Prince Alark of Samdagarh, welcomed him and promised him all help at an appropriate time to take revenge on the smuggler and restore his kingdom.

Salhes took a small army of forest dwellers and went in search of the man-eater. A little inside the forest he saw a young woman freshly killed and her husband crying by the side of her dead body. Salhes lifted the young man, consoled him and asked him to show the possible location of the man-eater. The young man was frightened beyond any measure but he led Salhes and his men to an area in the forest where the animal could be hiding. Salhes asked his men to surround the forest region from all sides and let loose the hounds. As the hounds progressed inside, Salhes could sense the tiger's movement. He quickly shot three arrows in succession and then sent one of his men to check what had happened. His aim had been perfect and the servant returned with the dead tiger whose mouth smelt of fresh human flesh. Soon a large black ape jumped to the ground from a tree there. It was also shot down. The young man whose wife had been killed recognized the ape as the dwarf ghost as had been labelled by the local population. Thus came the end of a terror unleashed by the man-eater and his companion ape.

Salhes's next target was to kill the demonized woman who had been going around the villages and killing people at random. While he was planning his expedition, he was visited by a sage who advised him to take the help of the Malin sisters. In particular, Kusma would be of immense help. The sage also described the features of the demon as a young woman of exceptional beauty who lived in a cave along with her pet wild animals. He gave him hints about the possible location of the cave in the mountains.

Salhes agreed and went alone to Yogini Cave to meet Kusma Malin. Kusma readily agreed to accompany Salhes to the hideout of the demonic woman. The two together travelled to the mountains and at a remote location found the woman playing with her pet tigers and wolves. As he pulled his bow to shoot the demon, Kusma held his hand and prevented him from shooting. She cautioned him saying that the real heroics lay in capturing the woman alive. She expected that the woman might be a psychic patient, suffering from some abnormalities; most likely one related to her suppressed sexual desires which had not been satisfied.

Salhes was surprised at Kusma's approach towards the enemy but she insisted that she understood women better. If the demonic woman got the company of a real strong man, who could fulfil her strong sexual urge, it was very likely that she would be reformed. Salhes then returned to make preparations so that an attack could be mounted to capture the demon alive. It needed a different tactic as she harbingered a lot of wild and ferocious animals who had long been used to killing human beings.

Salhes took Karikanha and his Bagh Garh army on an expedition to capture the demon alive. With the help of his tiger and bear, Salhes managed to corner the young woman and Karikanha overpowered her. While other wild animals ran away, a lone wolf, the best pet of all, kept her company. He was not harmed. For the first time in many years the young woman, who had developed such hatred towards humans to resort to mass killing, felt her strength failing under the strong arm of Karikanha. She closed her eyes in ecstasy and implored her captor to kill her by pressing his strong arms which would give her immense pleasure. But Kusma came quickly and calmed her down, cut her huge nails which acted as weapons, bathed her and dressed her well. Soon a princess-like young woman was standing in front of them, who looked at Karikanha as the man who could satisfy her desires. She could not recall her name but Kusma called her Aranya, one that was from the forest.

Salhes proposed that Karikanha should marry Aranya as he had found her getting attracted towards him. Karikanha had been unmarried so far and a good match had not been found yet. Kusma quickly arranged for the material for a Gandharva marriage then and there.

With the capture of the demon, Salhes had eliminated the threats to the lives of many villagers.

While the celebrations were going on for the marriage of Karikanha, Salhes's time for his Dwiragaman had arrived. As per the prevailing custom, his youngest brother Budheswar went to Virat Nagar to ask the king, Salhes's father-in-law, to agree to a particularly auspicious date and time for the dwiragaman when Salhes would come to take his wife to Mahisautha.

The Kirat king Sujong had by now gained strength and was on the lookout for an opportunity to humiliate Salhes. He got wind of the travel plan of Budheswar and his men intercepted Budheswar on his way to Virat Nagar, kidnapped him and brought him to Rangila Garh, the capital of Sujong's Kirat kingdom. Sujong sent a message to Salhes that he should come unarmed and surrender forthwith otherwise his younger brother would be hanged. This was a setback for Salhes but he was unfazed. Salhes knew that the real target for Sujong was not to keep Salhes captive but to gain control of the Malin sisters. Sujong knew very well the capabilities of the Malin sisters and wanted to have them as his wives.

As desired by Sujong, he travelled to Rangila Garh unarmed and got his brother released after surrendering himself to Sujong. He also quietly sent word with Budheswar to Kusma that under no circumstances any of the Malin sisters should get influenced by the lies spread by Sujong. He assured them that his captivity at Rangila Garh was a transient phase and he would find ways to free himself.

Sujong tried to threaten Salhes in various ways but Salhes would not bow to his demands. Sujong then decided to attack Virat Nagar and kidnap Salhes's wife Satyavati from there. For this, he sought help from several kings and accomplices. The king of Pakariya, Mān Chandra, was a weak person. He was dominated by his chief minister and military commander Chuhar Mall, a brave person with very long moustaches. Chuhar Mall was a famous burglar of Mokama, on the southern bank of river Ganga. He was greedy also and found the invitation of Sujong tempting. Although the kingdoms of Pakariya and Virat Nagar had been in friendly relations, Chuhar Mall decided to go with Sujong to invade Virat Nagar.

Even though Salhes had sent word for the Malin sisters not to surrender to Sujong to get him released, Kusma and Dona decided to go to Rangila Garh and play the drama of surrender to get access to the inner court and the palace of Sujong. Sujong was overjoyed to find Kusma and Dona but instead of freeing Salhes immediately after taking the two sisters captive, he decided to wait for a while till he completed his mission at Virat Nagar and brought Salhes's wife. Showing Satyavati along with Kusma and Dona in his captivity to Salhes would be to inflict a major humiliation on him and his morale would surely plummet. This was the reason that Sujong did not free Salhes even after finding Kusma and Dona within his grasp. He left for Virat Nagar with his army.

While Sujong was away, the two Malin sisters acted on a detailed plot to drug the security personnel of the prison, bribe the maids who were taking food for Salhes and make all the arrangements to cut the chains of Salhes. The plan was executed to the finest precision and Salhes walked free in the dead of night. A part of his army had already arrived at the palace gates. Quickly he overpowered all the security guards, put them into captivity along with all the inmates of the palace and appointed his men to various security positions. Thus while Sujong was still on his way to Virat Nagar to kidnap Salhes's wife, Salhes had taken over the Rangila Garh fort.

The battle at Virat Nagar was very intense. Sujong's Kirat army was aided by the armies of Samdagarh, led by the smuggler king Tarumall and of Pakariya, led by Chuhar Mall. Virat Nagar was being defended by its army, aided by the armies of Bagh Garh, led by Karikanha, and of Mahisautha, led by Budheswar. Prince Alark also went to fight along with Budheswar. In the fierce fighting, Tarumall was killed and Budheswar was badly injured.

While fighting was still going on, Salhes and Kusma arrived at Virat Nagar. While Kusma took care of Budheswar's wounds using her knowledge of herbs and medicinal plants, Salhes himself went into the battle to boost the morale of his army and those fighting to defend Virat Nagar. Chuhar Mall was taken captive in the battle with Salhes. Sujong's army was finally defeated and the king himself was taken captive. He along with Chuhar Mall was brought to Mahisautha by Salhes.

After the battle dust settled, Salhes brought his wife Satyavati from Virat Nagar to Mahisautha. King Mān Chandra of Pakariya arrived at Mahisautha and pleaded with Salhes to release Chuhar Mall. Salhes on the contrary, argued with Mān Chandra to use that opportunity and get rid of Chuhar Mall who was doing more harm than good to Pakariya. After Salhes promised him that he would take personal responsibility for the security of the kingdom of Pakariya from any revenge action taken by Chuhar Mall, reluctantly King Mān Chandra agreed to dismiss Chuhar Mall from his services.

Once dismissed from King's service, Chuhar Mall was released from prison. He went back to his home town Mokama on the southern bank of the river Ganga.

Salhes had to go to solve the problem of flooding due to water in Chakra Lake which was being controlled by a rogue Mahanth. He needed a month's time. During this period he deputed his nephew Karikanha to the security of the kingdom of Pakariya. Karikanha was very proud of his strength. Little did he realize that Chuhar Mall had spread a web of very trusted people among the security establishment in the kingdom. Chuahr knew every nook and corner of the palace and also the places where precious items had been kept. He had to take revenge on Salhes for forcing the Pakariya king to dismiss him. He decided to steal the precious Mahalata necklace, supposedly worth seven crores of gold coins, which the king had made for his only daughter to be gifted to her during marriage. He organized a band of expert burglars and set them on the job of digging several miles long tunnel from some faraway location up to the palace. The way this work was carried out, people thought wells were being dug for water. No one ever suspected what was going on. On the appointed date Karikanha was drugged on some pretext by the sub-ordinate security staff loyal to Chuhar Mall. When he fell asleep, the burglars carried out the job neatly, entering the palace and stealing the necklace they knew too well.

The next morning Karikanha was summoned by the king to explain what had happened. Karikanha was lost for words. He was held responsible for the theft and put behind bars.

Salhes came to know about the incident of burglary and Karikanha's arrest when he returned from his Chakra mission. He went to Pakariya and pleaded with the king to release Karikanha, assuring him that the necklace would surely be traced and brought back. Salhes told the king that it was a revenge act by Chuhar Mall and surely his men had been instrumental in stealing the necklace. The king, who by now had become antagonistic towards Salhes, was infuriated at this suggestion and did not want to allow Salhes a free hand in accusing Chuhar without any proof. He argued that Karikanha could be released only on the condition that Salhes himself stay in prison till the necklace was recovered. Salhes agreed and went into prison at Pakariya.

The news of Salhes's voluntary arrest was brought to the Malin sisters at the Yogini Cave by Salhes's wife herself. Kusma immediately thought of a plan, took about one hundred well-trained men along with horses and elephants and departed for Mokama. At Mokama she sent her spies to find out the whereabouts of Chuhar Mall. They brought the information that after getting dismissed from the Pakariya king's service, Chuhar Mall had taken to drinking and women in frustration. He had also begun attending the local casino and gambled heavily.

Dressed as a Nati (one from the nomadic tribe, in which women dress very differently with eye-catching blouses and frocks) Kusma befriended a local dancing girl, who was also a bar owner. She introduced herself as a dancing queen from the Himalayas. She performed some dancing moves to show that she did indeed know very novel dances which would attract a large number of customers to the bar and increase her business manyfold. The local dancing girl was very impressed with Kusma and with the help of her men went on to advertise the special performance of a Himalayan dancer.

The dance program was a hit with many rich customers attending the performance along with Chuhar Mall. Kusma then asked Chuhar to sit with her on the gambling table. Chuhar was in the habit of placing large bets. Kusma acted as if she was losing and after a few moves, she declared that she had lost all her money. But she would not leave the table. She set herself on the bet. If the opponent won, he would be entitled to spend a night with her. Chuhar was completely dazed at the beauty of Kusma and he fell for the bet. Surely Kusma lost again and offered to spend the night with him in a special room. The room had been prearranged by her accomplices. Chuhar was taken to the room by Kusma herself and seated on a bed. Kusma began serving him the best drinks available there. The drinks had been spiked as planned. Kusma praised Chuhar for his acts of bravery and burglary and raised the subject of Mahalata necklace which Chuhar had successfully brought with him. Chuhar was losing his senses. He blurted out the location of the necklace where he had hidden it along with other burgled items. Soon he became unconscious and fell asleep on the bed.

Kusma quickly went with her accomplices and dug out the necklace. She also managed to cut the long moustaches of Chuhar with a sharp razor and kept them in safe custody. As it had been preplanned, she immediately left Mokama on a special boat to cross the river Ganga. A set of horses and elephants were waiting on the other bank of the river. The contingent left under heavy security for Pakariya.

In the King's court, Kusma announced that the Mahalata necklace had been retrieved and the thief also had been identified.

She told the king to assemble the full court with all the ministers and courtesans and also bring Salhes from captivity. Although the king was apprehensive of the tall claim, he ordered Salhes to be brought to the court but in chains. The entire court was overflowing with even common citizens thronging there to have a look at the thief and the stolen item.

Kusma carefully presented the king with the necklace on a platter. The king laughed and said, "That's what I had always thought. The necklace had been stolen by Karikanha himself and after he was freed from here, you people brought the necklace accompanied by a lot of drama. What is so great about retrieving the stolen material when the chief of security himself was the thief?"

Kusma then carefully opened another platter covered with a silk cloth. There was a pair of long moustaches belonging to Chuhar Mall. She asked the king and the entire court, "Who does not recognize this moustache?"

The entire court was stunned. Kusma added, "If anyone still has doubts, I am ready to take the person to Mokama and show how Chuhar Mall looks now and also the place where he had hidden the necklace burgled from the palace." Pin-drop silence fell in the court. The king bowed his head in shame. Salhes, still in chains, told the king, "Even after you dismissed him from your service, you remained loyal to Chuhar Mall, a person who was a thug and a thief all along. You instead doubted our security arrangements and cast aspersions on the faithfulness of an honest person like Karikanha. Now that Chuhar Mall has been exposed, I beseech you to remove any fear of him from your mind and rule this Pakariya kingdom with our assistance. We shall always be available to protect you from any future misadventure of Chuhar Mall".

The king was demoralized. He had no words. He obeyed Salhes, got his chains unfastened and offered his daughter to his youngest brother Budheswar in marriage. The two kingdoms were finally united in marital bonds. Brave Salhes, with the help of Kusma, was immortalized and is worshipped even today.

Even though Salhes and his wife Satyavati requested Kusma to stay in Mahisautha along with her sisters, she preferred the Yogini cave. The four sisters remained mentally devoted to Salhes for their entire life although their pledge, taken at the tender age of twelve years, to become the wives of Salhes, was never fulfilled.

* * *

II

Lorik Maniyar

[The story of Lorik Maniyar is also referred to as the story of Sati Mañjari, his devout, chaste and virtuous wife. It is said that whatever Lorik achieved was because of the power of Mañjari's chastity and virtuousness. People treated her as an incarnation of Goddess Durga herself.

Scholars believe this popular tale to belong to the eleventh century AD when anarchy prevailed after the decline of Buddhism and with the rising influence of Sanatan Dharma. Mithila was badly divided into several smaller kingdoms, each being ruled by cruel, adulterous kings who treated womenfolk like slaves. Lorik attained fame because even though he did not have any princely or aristocratic lineage and came from a very humble background of a milkman's family, he eliminated those cruel kings with his strength and helped the general populace lead a peaceful life. The folk story of Lorik is one of the most respected stories immortalized through ballads.]

A king, Ughara Pamar, ruled the village of Gaura. He was cruel to the core and almost demonic in his treatment of young women. He kept a large number of beautiful young women in his harem as captives. In addition, he had made a rule that the first four nights of any freshly married woman would be compulsorily spent in his bed. Only unmarried girls had been spared as he had been told by an astrologer that kidnapping maidens would invite bad luck for him. For fear of Ughara, very few girls in that village used to ever get married. Some fourteen hundred girls of marriageable age were unmarried. (See Box for the original narration in Maithili.) However, he used to visit fairs and other gatherings and mark beautiful girls whom he would kidnap the night they got married. He had a large army and several strong fighter-wrestlers under his command, notable among them being Sonika and Monika.

राम जाने गोसइआँ जाने ईशर भगवान
तखनी बोलैए माँजरि मोहिब
सुनलनि मैआ बुढिया धरम के कुछ बात
हमर गाम मे छैक राजा उघरा पमार
जतेक गमरू अबै बियाहए लए एहि गाम
ओकरे डर से कियो ने करै गौरा बियाह
तैं चौदह सए कनिआ कुमारि छै ढठिसार

Ram knows and know other Gods
Mānjari then speaks to the Goddess
Listen Mother some facts about the culture
Ughara Pamar is the king in my village
Whosoever comes to marry in this village
No one marries here because of his fear
Fourteen hundred maidens are unmarried here

Among many such marked girls was the only daughter of a well-to-do farmer Mahar, who owned a hundred thousand cows. The girl, Mānjari, was an exceptional beauty and devoted to Mother Durga, whom she worshipped daily in the temple at Habi-Pattan. She would always seek Mother Goddess's blessings to protect her from the evil eyes of Ughara Pamar in her prayers.

Mānjari was a virtuous, generous, and chaste maiden whom people would call Durga for her devotion to the Goddess. The stories about Mānjari's exceptional beauty had spread far and wide. She was also very kind and empathetic to all types of creatures. She had once saved a dying crow from the attack of a kite. The crow, now called Bajali, grew in her protection. She took pity on a lame orphan girl and gave shelter to her. She was a constant companion to Mānjari. The lame girl, called Lurki, was very intelligent and brave.

Mānjari's father had decided to marry her to a man who would protect her from Ughara Pamar. This was no small requirement. Mānjari's maternal uncle, Sevachan, had been entrusted with the responsibility to find a suitable match. Sevachan travelled far and wide for years, so much so that he broke several pairs of slippers. Finally, he learnt about the Silhat wrestling arena in Agaura village which was famous as the place for the wrestling practices by the best wrestlers.

Agaura village was very large, extending 28 miles across, the ruler was King Sahdeo. His son, Prince Mahadeo was still unmarried. A plump fellow with little fighting acumen and strength, he would only indulge in eating and resting. King Sahdeo had a beautiful daughter, Chanain, who was married to Prince Shivadhar of Boha.

When Sevachan arrived in Agaura village, he did not know where to go. He was led to the king's court. There he expressed his desire to find a suitable match for his niece. King Sahdeo offered his son, Mahadeo. When Sevachan looked at Mahadeo, he was utterly disappointed. He thought, "This plump guy will simply run away at the very sight of Ughara Pamar." He told King Sahdeo to guide him to Silhat arena. The king got angry, proclaimed that no one should tell the stranger anything about Silhat and drove him away.

Sevachan was disappointed but did not lose hope. Finally, with the help of a washerwoman, he was led to the Silhat arena, where already several wrestlers were busy in their practices. Among them was one Lorik Maniyar, son of a poor ploughman Kubbe. Maniyar had been added to his name signifying his shining forehead with valour and bravery, like the snake of the same name, which carried a gemstone on its head.

Kubbe used to work in the King's fields and also graze the cows of the entire village. He had got two sons, Lorik and Sabar, as a blessing from Mother Durga to whom he was intensely devoted.

Lorik was a heroic wrestler of unmatched strength and valour. He had a pole axe weighing some eighty mounds which he carried all the time with him. When he walked it looked as if a mountain peak was moving. When he patted his thighs as a challenge to anyone in the wrestling arena, trees would be uprooted by the vibrations produced. If he walked briskly, the earth would begin shaking. When he laughed people felt as if a thunder had occurred. His axe always shone brilliantly. Lorik had vowed to Mother Durga that he would always protect women, cows and anyone in distress. Rajal Washerman, Baru Dushadh and Bantha Chamar were his friends at the arena and themselves brave men.

Sevachan was mesmerized at the sight of Lorik. He also was a celebrated wrestler. He tested Lorik and was convinced that this person could be a killer of Ughara Pamar. He went and talked to his father about the marriage proposal of Lorik with Mānjari. After some negotiations it was settled and a date was fixed. Sevachan returned happily.

On the day of the marriage people in Agaura village were invited to join the marriage party going to Gaura village. Many of the villagers, knowing the trouble they might face due to Ughara Pamar, backed out. Only the select brave men accompanied Lorik. On the way towards late afternoon, they reached a place where a large number of washermen were cleaning the clothes of Ughara Pamar's royal household. The marriage party asked them to loan them the dresses for a day which they would return when going back from the marriage ceremony. The washermen did not oblige. They were beaten and driven away, their clothes snatched and all the members had royal dresses on them. Further on they reached a bazaar where they wanted to eat something. They were denied even on payment because of Ughara's orders to shopkeepers. They looted the shops and not only had their stomach filled with good dishes, but they also found a lot of precious gems and jewels which they took with them.

Finally, they arrived near the bride's house and put up temporarily in a mango orchard as per the local custom. Here the first to arrive there, as part of the reception for the marriage party, were a gathering of women asking for '*gua-pan*' from the groom's father as per the prevailing custom (one of the rituals before formally commencing marriage, as a token of approval from the groom's side). However, these women had daggers tied to their saris at the back. Soon it was discovered that they were a bunch of male warriors disguised as women, sent by Ughara Pamar to decimate the marriage party. But the brave men, all veterans of that famous Silhat arena, quickly overpowered all of them and punished them. Some died and others fled the scene.

In due course, the marriage was solemnised, and the marriage party had their feast of the choicest food in whatever quantity whosoever desired. The bride and the groom went to their nuptial chamber decorated elegantly for the occasion. After the initial courtship, Lorik fell asleep, keeping his heavy axe in a corner. But Mānjari lay wide awake as she was very afraid. Even though in the arms of such a brave husband, she was shivering as if it was very cold. She could not sleep as she was sure Ughara would leave nothing to chance to kidnap her as per his wishes.

Two of Ughara's best fighters, Sonika and Monika, were sent for this purpose. Dressed in saris, they reached early and mingled with womenfolk as friends of Mānjari without speaking anything. When everyone went to retire after the marriage, they began giving shape to their plan. They went up the roof of the straw hut which was the nuptial chamber, cut a portion and Sonika entered the room from the top carrying a sword. Being wide awake, Mānjari saw him and was scared to death. She tried to awaken Lorik by shaking him but he did not respond. Time was running out. She then took a strand of her hair and placed it near Lorik's nose. This awakened him. By that time Sonika came very close to the bed and was almost on the body of Lorik. Lorik shook his body so violently that not only Sonika fell down but his sword was also thrown away. Lorik was still unarmed. He looked for his axe. But that was in a corner obstructed by Sonika. Strangely Mānjari quickly leaped and picked up the heavy axe from that corner. As soon as Lorik got his axe, Sonika's head was separated from his body and the blood oozing from the corpse filled the entire room. Thinking it was getting late for Sonika to come out with Mānjari, Monika tried to enter the room from the top. He too was cut into two pieces.

Thus the first night was spent in action but Ughara's designs had been defeated. So far Mānjari was safe. The next day it was the auspicious occasion for her to depart, along with the marriage party, to her husband's village. As per local custom, Lorik's father asked for the gifts. But Mānjari's father explained to him, "The tradition in our village is not to give any specific gift to the returning marriage party. You ask your son to throw a stick as far as he can. The entire cattle, cows, goats, even donkeys and pigs grazing in the area surrounded by that distance will be yours. You carry them along."

Lorik came forward and threw a stick which landed some fourteen *kos* (28 miles) away. They collected all the cattle as promised and departed along with Mānjari in a decorated new palanquin in the middle of a set of brave men. Mānjari took Bājali crow and the maid Lurki along with her. Lurki carried a long wooden pestle in her hand.

Lorik's younger brother took charge of all the cows, goats were in charge of Bantha Chamar (shoemaker), donkeys with Rajal Dhobi (washerman) and the pigs were driven by Baru Kotwal, all friends of Lorik at the Silhat arena. Lorik himself, armed with his heavy pole axe, was walking behind the palanquin to protect Mānjari from any untoward incident.

In the morning Ughara Pamar also learnt about the death of his two very strong fighters at the hands of Lorik. Although momentarily feeling incapacitated, he gathered courage, assembled another army of fighter-wrestlers and decided to attack the returning convoy of the marriage party to kidnap Mañjari. It would be a shame for him if a freshly married girl, even though very young and not yet fit to satisfy his bed urge, were allowed to leave the village. This had never happened since the time he took charge of the crown.

As the marriage party came near a thick jungle, they were surrounded by the fighters of Ughara. There was very little time to react. But the brave men attacked with such ferocity that Ughara's men had to retreat. At this stage, Ughara himself came forward and attacked Lorik. There was a fierce bout of wrestling fight between the two warriors. In the end, Lorik managed to kill Ughara and thus came to end a reign of terror unleashed on the newly married women in Gaura village.

Back in Agaura village, King Sahdeo's daughter, Chanain, although married for several years and now in full youth, missed her husband. She learnt that her husband had become impotent because of a curse of God Indra. She got a promise from him that their marriage stood annulled and she was now free to find a suitable man for her. But who? She would be going against the wishes of her father and needed protection. She could not accept anyone. The person had to be strong and brave to protect her and defend in all adverse circumstances. She set her eyes on Lorik.

Lorik was a well-developed young man but his newlywed wife, Mañjari, was still an adolescent. She was not mature enough for his sexual needs. She had been married at that early age because of the fear of the prying eyes of Ughara Pamar. She was, however, an epitome of piousness, chastity and virtuousness.

Lorik was sent a word from Chanain through a trusted maid to meet her in the dead of night through a backdoor. Lorik took the bait. They met at the appointed hour and Lorik immediately fell for Chanain. Both needed each other. They enjoyed love-making as mature lovers. The secret meetings became almost a regular affair.

After a few months, when their secret meetings became common knowledge in the neighbourhood, Chanain proposed to Lorik to run away to some unknown distant place. Lorik agreed as he could afford to leave his legal wife for some years still. Chanain took her valuable possessions and accompanied Lorik in the dead of night. But they were stopped by Baru, an arena mate of Lorik, who was on sentry duty at the palace. Lorik reasoned with Baru that he had embraced Chanain after she was deserted by her impotent husband. Not honouring the invitation of a young desirous woman would have been tantamount to doubting his manhood. Although Baru did not dispute this version, he insisted that they could not elope when he was on sentry duty, lest he would be hanged along with his family members by King Sahdeo. Lorik suggested to Baru to leave the services of King Sahdeo and join King Harba-Barba of Nyorigarh, who had sought his services on many occasions. Baru agreed and allowed them to leave. He quit the place in the night and went to the kingdom of Harba-Barba.

Lorik and Chanain reached Hardi Than and took shelter there in the house of one shopkeeper. After a few days, word went around that an extremely beautiful young woman had arrived with a stranger in the village. The local king, Mochani, wanted her in his harem. He laid traps for Lorik to be killed somehow. He sent for him and when he arrived, gave him a letter in the name of his military commander, a fighter-wrestler par excellence, Gaj Bhimmal, who was at a remote location. The letter had instructions for Gaj Bhimmal to kill Lorik. Somehow Chanain managed to read the letter. She asked her lover to go and get one horse from the King, which no one ever rode and desired. After a few attempts, when the horses brought by Lorik were rejected by Chanain, Lorik finally brought a horse, named Katra, a discard for all purposes. This is what Chanain desired. When this horse was taken care of, he proved to be a protector for Lorik, as if sent from heaven.

Lorik now knew that Gaj Bhimmal would try to kill him. When he reached the arena and gave the letter to Gaj Bhimmal, before Gaj Bhimmal could even finish reading, his head was severed by the pole axe of Lorik. Lorik sent the head to King Mochani. Mochani was devastated but soon composed himself. He allowed the event to cool for a few days and thought of another plan. He again called Lorik and gave him a letter to be delivered to King Harba of Nyorigarh, who was a fast friend of King Mochani. The content was the same: severe the bearer's head and send that to me.

King Harba was notorious for his ill-treatment of other kings he had defeated in various battles. He had kept them in special cells where daily torture was routinely inflicted. He was equally notorious for keeping beautiful young women in his harem. He had made two Brahman sisters, Duhbi-Suhbi, his special concubines. His younger brother Barba was his military commander and he had another brave fighter wrestler named Ghughara Pamar, brother of Ughara Pamar. When Ughara died, Ghughara fled and took shelter in Nyorigarh. King Harba's nephew, Prince Angar of Kotharam Garh, was an expert in handling the fire arrows and also a master of using *Brahmaphansh* (a trap used to entrap enemies). No one knew how to break loose from the *Brahmaphansh* once trapped inside.

When Lorik arrived near the kingdom of Nyorigarh, he was met by Ghughara Pamar. Lorik introduced himself and asked for the King's palace. He also told him that he was carrying a letter from King Mochani to King Harba who wanted to kill him (Lorik) and send his head back. Ghughara knew the strength of Lorik who had killed his brother Ughara. At the same time, he was tempted to attempt to kill Lorik himself to get a big reward from the king. He played a trick and told Lorik to wait under a shaded tree till he came back after informing the king. Lorik dismounted, left his horse Katra to graze around and lay under the tree shade. Soon he fell asleep. Ghughara was hiding nearby. He went stealthily and took away Lorik's pole axe. He tried to run but carrying such a heavy axe was difficult. In the meantime, Katra sensed something amiss and hit Lorik to awaken him. Although irritated at being disturbed in his sleep, Lorik woke up and was surprised to find his axe missing. He could find the footprint on the grass as, being unable to lift the heavy axe, Ghughara had carried it by dragging it on the grass. He immediately followed the trail on his horse. Ghughara had not gone far when he was caught. A fierce battle took place between unarmed Lorik and armed Ghughara. Lorik tried to save himself from the attacks till once he succeeded in kicking Ghughara so hard that the axe fell on the ground. With lightning speed, Lorik lifted his axe and cut Ghughara into two. Thus came the end of a rogue.

There was commotion all around when villagers discovered Ghughara lying in a pool of blood. The news of Ghughara's killing reached King Harba. He became furious and asked his brother Barba, his military commander to catch and punish whosoever was the killer of Ghughara. Lorik still lay resting under the same tree, not knowing how to reach the King's quarters. Barba surrounded the area with his men. It was morning. Lorik had just returned from the river after taking a bath and cleaning the horse. He looked at the horse who got an opportunity to show his war skills. Lorik mounted the horse and ran through the army shaking his axe as far as possible on all sides. The horse was moving forward, kicking men behind and also biting some in front. Lorik went slaying the men on the sides. Finally, he came directly in front of Barba who was also riding an equally trained war horse. A fierce battle took place but Barba was no match for Lorik's tactics and strength. After a long struggle, Lorik slew Barba's head with his axe. The remaining men took to their heels.

After losing his brother, King Harba sent for his nephew Prince Angar with a promise of gift of several villages if he could kill Lorik. The young wife of the prince tried to persuade him not to go as she knew Lorik was not an ordinary fighter. But the prince would not listen. His *Brahmaphansh* trap had so far never failed. He was confident of trapping his enemy.

The men were so afraid of Lorik that when the Prince arrived and asked for a guide to the hiding place of Lorik, no one came forward. Finally, it was left to the sentry Baru, an old mate of Lorik to accompany Prince Angar to the place where Lorik rested. The prince began shooting his fire arrows throwing the forest into fire. Lorik sensed some trouble and along with his horse jumped into the river nearby. After the fire subsided, he came out and went to fight Prince Angar. But soon he was trapped along with the horse. Prince Angar laughed aloud and started abusing Lorik. He told him that he was in no hurry to kill him, rather would allow Lorik to die a slow death in the trap. Lorik found that the more he tried to free himself, the more the trap became tighter and tighter around his body. Prince Angar also began saying bad words about the reputation of Lorik's wrestling arena Silhat. Baru was standing nearby feeling helpless. Even though an old mate of Lorik, he was now in the service of King Harba and could not go against the King. But when he found his arena being abused, he decided to do something. He signalled to Lorik to use his teeth at a particular spot of the trap. As soon as Lorik held that joint with his teeth, the trap loosened. Before Prince Angar could realise what had happened, Lorik was up on his feet with the axe in his hand. The next moment the prince lay on the ground in two pieces.

King Harba then himself took to the battle with whatever men remained in his army. But the army was already demoralised and could not stand Lorik's onslaught. In the end, Harba was also killed. Lorik then went to the palace with Baru and freed all the prisoners. He assured the womenfolk that no harm would be done to them. Lorik divided the kingdom into first two and then again one half into two. The first half he gave to the queen widow, one quarter to the Duhbi-Suhbi sisters and one quarter to his friend Baru Chowkidar.

When Lorik was engaged in fighting with Harba-Barba, Chanain was left alone. She was forced to go to the court of King Mochani. The king was waiting desperately to take her to bed. As there was no Lorik around, he had nothing to fear. However, Chanain was an intelligent woman and she knew how to defend herself. She made herself up beautifully and appeared before the king with drinks. She explained, "Before going to bed with you, this is my only wish that I should pour a couple of pegs for your Excellency. The king was so enamoured that he could not refuse. He drove away all the maids and others. Chanain was alone. The king had kept the sword at his side. While the king sipped his drink, made more intoxicating with the hands of Chanain, she began a suggestive dance. The king was almost floored. He could not keep count of the number of pegs he drank. As he fell almost unconscious, Chanain took the sword and severed his head, quietly came out and left the palace without anyone's knowledge.

The palace was in shock. No one dared pursue Chanain. When Lorik returned and learned about the entire episode, he was very proud of the intelligence of Chanain. They went inside the palace, assured everyone of fair treatment and began living there. Chanain bore one son to him.

The days were passing gaily. He was absorbed in the love of Chanain but would sometimes recall Mānjari, and become restless. He knew that by that time Mānjari must have grown into a youthful woman and expected her husband. Chanain was however envious of Mānjari.

Mānjari was living in her husband's house like a devout woman, practising all the religious acts which the local custom demanded. She would worship Goddess Durga daily. By now Lorik's younger brother was married. Mānjari had a companion as a sister-in-law. They together tended to their father-in-law and mother-in-law who had grown old.

Mānjari decided to send a message to Lorik. She had no idea where to find him. She wrote a letter and tied it to the foot of the crow Bājali and instructed him to deliver only to Lorik, cautioning him that in no case should the letter fall in the hands of Chanain. The crow flew away.

Bājali managed to reach Hardi Than and locate Lorik. But he observed that most of the time Lorik was accompanied by Chanain. He waited. Finally once when Chanain went to take a bath, he descended and perched himself on Lorik's arm. Lorik was surprised but quickly recognised the crow. The clever crow immediately turned his foot with the letter towards his face. Lorik unfastened the letter and called a reader to decipher the contents. After he knew what was written there, he became restless. He immediately ordered his army to prepare and proceed to Agaura at the earliest. Chanain was unhappy. She asked him to test the chastity of Mānjari, as she doubted that in so many years with youthful age, Mānjari must have found someone to entertain her in bed. Lorik was confident of the chastity of his wife but to quieten Chanain, he arranged for the test when they arrived in Agaura. Mānjari was told to prove her chastity.

The whole village assembled near the Durga temple. Mānjari took a bath in the river, worshipped Mother Durga and dressed in her best silk finery she sat beside a dried sandalwood tree in the temple compound and meditated. Suddenly fire erupted from the corner of her sari and engulfed the entire tree. Flames leapt sky high. The whole tree was burnt but Mānjari sat there completely unharmed. The whole village stood in silence praying for Mānjari. She came out unscathed and proved her chastity.

Mānjari had absolutely no malice towards Chanain. She welcomed her son also as her own. Lorik was now devoted to Mānjari. Although still envious in her heart, Chanain had to accept that she alone could not be the master of Lorik's love for all her life. The terrorising kings had all been eliminated one by one. In all, Lorik fought thirty-six fierce battles against the social tyrants of his time. He is revered even today as a hero among the milkmen to which caste he belonged.

* * *

III

Raiya Ranpal

[The story of Raiya Ranpal, encompassing two generations, the King Arindam Ranpal of Vasampur and his son Gugli, is sung by the Pamariya tribe in Mithila. The Pamariyas are Muslims and they earn their livelihood by descending on the household where a son is newly born. They sing the story of Ranpal and please the members of the household and in return get good gifts in the form of cash, clothes and other valuables. The Pamariya tribes' activities are now on the decline as the young members seek modern occupation and also the society does not give them due credit.

The tale corresponds to the Middle Ages, around 8-9th centuries AD, when Mithila was divided into many small kingdoms, kings fighting among themselves and also addicted to alcohol and women. The weakness of these kings led to the spread of Islam. Also, the decadence of the Hindu religion setting in the society was providing a fertile ground for people to embrace Islam. King Arindam Ranpal, the last of the kings of the Pal dynasty is considered as the saviour of Hindu society by fighting the invading Muslims and driving them away.]

Part-1 : Ranpal

King Pradyot Narayan of Ghatampur had two wives. He had seven sons from his first wife and only one daughter from his second wife, Queen Kuntala. After the death of the king, his sons tried to drive away their stepmother and disinherit her from the property of the kingdom. But Queen Kuntala was not only clever but a brave lady who had mastered the warfare techniques. She revolted and threatened for war. The Ghatampur (referred in short as Ghatam and mostly as Ghatma in the ballads) king then gave her a small share and the fort at Sihulagarh which was also surrounded by the dense Sihula forest on three sides and a river on the other side. She left for Sihulagarh along with her daughter Princess Yasomati. The princess was also as brave as beautiful and well-versed in horse riding and handling the weaponry for warfare.

The Ghatam king, led by the eldest brother Narpati, did not care for just rules for their subjects. Instead, they engaged in acts of robbery, kidnapping and wanton killing. He had become almost a puppet of the Muslim chieftain Himmat Mirza whose sole aim was to spread terror and force people to convert to Islam. He expected due reward for his jihadi acts by the Nawabs in Delhi.

During one such raid by the Ghatam king on the kingdom of Vipulgarh, the combined army of Mirza and Narpati had killed the king Vipuldev who didn't have a strong army and plundered the entire kingdom. The plunder also consisted of thousands of beautiful young women who were to be taken to Benaras to be sold in the slave and prostitution market there by Sripati, the youngest prince of Ghatampur. The town of Shovangarh, where the kingdom's richest trader Shovan Sahu resided, had also been looted of its wealth. In addition, Shovan Sahu got a ransom call of five crore gold coins to be given to the Ghatma king.

Raiya (colloquial for Raja or King) Ranpal came to know of the misfortune befalling the kingdom of Vipulgarh and took his army of five thousand men to help them. Late in the evening when the victorious army was celebrating, the Ranpal army attacked them so unexpectedly and suddenly with such a force that not many had a chance to run away, neither were they in any position to fight. Ranpal's army also surrounded the party going to Benaras and freed all the women. They were allowed to go home. In the melee, Sripati was badly injured. The Princess Vasumati of Vipulgarh, who was also one of the women being taken to Benaras, took pity on him and ran away carrying him on her shoulder to a distant safe place where she took shelter in the house of a stranger. She didn't know whether the invading army was a friend or a foe. Two younger brothers of Narpati were taken prisoner. The Ranpal army got back almost everything which had been plundered. Order was established in Vipulgarh. The Ranpal army protected the entire Vipulgarh population.

Ranpal went to personally meet Shovan Sahu and asked him to construct, on a war footing, a fort near his town Shovangarh. He assured him of all help and also told him not to worry about the ransom demand from the Ghatma king as the Ghatmas would not dare enter Vipulgarh again till his army remained there. It was learnt that Shovan Sahu's wife and daughter had gone to Vaidyanatha Dham (a famous pilgrimage near the town of Deoghar in present-day Jharkhand) and while returning had been held back near Mokama on the southern bank of the river Ganga. They were staying in one of the *dharmashalas* (free inns on roadsides for the use of pilgrims) constructed by Shovan Sahu himself.

Ranpal found out the young prince Rangdev, the only son of Vipuldev and made him the king of Vipulgarh, keeping his overall protection. Among the persons missing after taking account of the dead in Vipulgarh, were the princess Vasumati of Vipulgarh and the youngest prince Sripati of Ghatampur. That was worrying for Ranpal and he sent his men all around to find them out.

After order was established, he released the two Ghatma princes who had been taken into custody on that fateful night and sent them with full honour back to Ghatampur. Even then Narpati would not rest in peace. He planned to kidnap the mother-daughter duo from the bank of river Ganga to take revenge for the defeat at Vipulgarh and sent two of his younger brothers to carry out the job. The kidnapping was a success and a message was sent to Shovan Sahu for a ransom of five crore gold coins for releasing them. However, before the kidnappers could go very far they were surrounded by men shouting "Long Live Ranpal" and were ambushed. The men accompanying the Ghatma princes fled hither and thither. The two Ghatma princes were taken into custody and Shovan Sahu's wife and daughter were sent to their home under full protection of a bunch of Ranpal's men. He appointed one of his best men, Maha Bhairav, as the military chief in charge of Vipulgarh and another dreaded soldier Bakka Dhangar as the chief around the Shovangarh area.

The house where Princess Vasumati had taken shelter with injured Sripati belonged to a poor family. However, the caretaker woman had a good knowledge of local herbs. Vasumati found some money in the purse carried by the Ghatma prince and she used them to buy provisions and medicines for the treatment of Sripati's wounds. The woman would bring strange herbs and apply them to the wounds of the prince. This had a miraculous effect. Princess Vasumati knew they were not safe in that small household. Strange as it might sound, knowing fully well that the prince was her father's enemy, she developed amorous feelings towards him. After a few days when the condition of the prince improved, she requisitioned a horse for herself and a palanquin for the prince by paying money to the house owner. She changed into disguise and left the place with the prince being carried in the palanquin. She kept moving towards Sihulagarh, hoping to find some sympathy with Queen Kuntala.

It so happened that Ranpal himself had been travelling with a small bunch of his trusted men in the same direction. He intercepted the palanquin and the horse rider and asked them about their identity and purpose of travel. During the small conversation, Ranpal recognised Princess Vasumati and requested her to go back to Vipulgarh with his men. He explained to her that full peace and order had been restored there and she had nothing to worry about. But she insisted that she would not leave the injured Sripati because she loved him and she would rather die with him if anything untoward happened. After much argument and counter-argument, Ranpal sent both of them to Vipulgarh with his men, along with advice to young king Rangdev to get his sister married to Sripati in full regal style as per their family tradition, although not inviting the Ghatmas, and send them to Ghatampur with full honour. Ranpal himself left for an unknown destination all alone.

The work on the construction of the fort, Shovangarh continued in full swing. Himmat Mirza was very disappointed having lost his plots and blamed the Ghatma king Narpati for poor military organisation and inefficiency in execution. However, he did not openly utter his frustration as he knew he had to depend on the Ghatmas. For his next attempt, he requisitioned five thousand cavalrymen from the Nawab of Aneesabad by agreeing to pay seven lakh gold coins. He ordered Narpati to arrange for the gold coins and also take care of the food and shelter of that army. Narpati obliged only too willingly. They waited for an opportune moment to attack Vipulgarh again.

Ranpal was captured by Princess Yasomati and her men while resting in the dense Sihula forest after travelling for a long time. He was deemed to be an enemy of the Ghatampur kingdom. He was taken to Sihulagarh and kept as a prisoner in the palace itself, getting somewhat better treatment compared to common prisoners.

While in captivity Ranpal was regularly visited by Queen Kuntala and her daughter Princess Yasomati. Ranpal confided to the Queen that he was extremely worried about the way the Ghatma king had been colluding with the Muslim chieftain Himmat Mirza whose sole aim was to spread terror and lure people to convert to Islam. He discussed at length with the Queen how decadence within the Hindu religion, leading to untouchability, social inequality, strict adherence to purity of action about rituals and customs and turning people into outcasts at the slightest deviation had provided a good opportunity for Islam. Untouchables and outcasts were embracing Islam and finding solace there. They would act as nuclei for further conversion. This had led several villages to convert to Islam and Mirza had been able to set up his empire and named it Mirzapur. The Queen would listen to these arguments patiently and agree with the observations of Ranpal. She hailed him as the real hero among the kings. Silently but surely Princess Yasomati had fallen in love with the prisoner Ranpal.

When Narpati learnt that Ranpal had been taken prisoner by his stepmother, he came calling and requested the Queen to hand over the prisoner, who was certainly the biggest enemy of the entire Ghatma clan and their kingdom. But the Queen differed with him on handing over the prisoner and no matter how much Narpati pleaded; the prisoner was not handed over to him. He threatened the Queen with dire consequences for sheltering an enemy of the kingdom.

Himmat Mirza's army along with reinforcements from the Nawab of Aneesabad had been regrouping in collaboration with the Ghatma army and planned to attack both Vipulgarh and Shovangarh simultaneously. They slowly moved towards Vipulgarh and Shovangarh, with the Ghatma army mainly focussing on the Shovangarh part while Mirza himself concentrated around Vipulgarh. Ranpal's absence from Vipulgarh had given them a good opportunity to attack and succeed. Secretly Mirza also wanted to annexe the Ghatma kingdom and further on set his eyes on Sihulagarh to marry Yasomati, whose fame as a brave woman had spread far and wide. But he publicly did not declare his intentions to Narpati.

Ranpal's military chief in charge of Vipulgarh, Maha Bhairav, sent him a message through a trained kite about the developments. The news made Ranpal restless. He sent a message to Queen Kuntala pleading for a temporary release from captivity to fight the enemy formation around Vipulgarh. He promised that after the battle he would be back all by himself into captivity. The Queen smiled at the honest person and gladly ordered his release for the greater good of the Hindu religion and society.

Ranpal rode his mare Ranjhampa and arrived at Vipulagarh to the astonishment of the Ghatma king. But the Ghatma king was more than surprised when Ranpal also ordered the release of the two Ghatma princes, Harpati and Surpati amid the battle, who had been taken captive during raids to liberate the wife and daughter of Shovan Sahu when they had been kidnapped for ransom. He specifically instructed that the prisoners should not be harmed in any manner at all and be given full respect.

While Mirza's men had to bear the attack of Maha Bhairav's tactical moves, Ghatma king was happily moving and fighting small skirmishes around Shovangarh. However, their joys were short-lived. Bakka Dhangar moved swiftly and forced the Ghatma army to retreat on the pain of losing heavily both men and ammunition. On the Vipulgarh front, Ranpal himself supervised the operation along with Maha Bhairav. The men Mirza had so proudly requisitioned could not bear the severity of the attack and they took to their heels. The main difference was in the attitude of the two fighting armies; one was defending a native land from outside attack and the other was simply engaged in capturing for the sake of self-promotion. The shout of "Long Live Ranpal" created such fear among Mirza's men that they thought it better to save their lives than to die for Mirza's ambitious plans. In the operation, Ranpal's men captured the richest young trader of Ghatampur, Manchan, who was ferrying supplies for the Mirza army as per instructions of Ghatma king Narpati.

After the enemy armies went back Ranpal returned to Sihulagarh as promised. Here he was given a warm welcome as by now Queen Kuntala had decided to marry her daughter to him. The news reached the Ghatampur kingdom as well as Mirza's camp.

Mirza had lost the battle but was not devoid of ideas. His main concern was a living Ranpal. He asked Narpati to pretend to mend fences with his stepmother so that he could access Ranpal and his wife Yasomati as his close relatives after marriage. This would help in planning his next move to eliminate Ranpal and then make a smooth takeover of the territories guarded by him. Narpati was too eager to oblige Mirza to take revenge on Ranpal. He sent emissaries to Sihulagarh expressing his joy at the news of the planned wedding of Princess Yasomati with King Ranpal. Although Queen Kuntala was suspicious, she did not show any unpleasantness with the emissaries. In due course, the marriage was solemnised and Ranpal with his wife went to live in the Shovangarh fort.

Several springs and summers passed peacefully. Trade and agriculture boomed. People were finally happy to find some peace from the constant fear of Mirza's attacks. The captive trader Manchan of Ghatampur was an eligible bachelor and he was found to be a perfect match for the daughter of Shovan Sahu. Ranpal himself talked to Shovan Sahu about this possibility because Shovan's daughter was now grown up and had to be married. Manchan had heard about the beautiful and intelligent daughter of Shovan Sahu and secretly desired her as his wife. When Ranpal brought the proposal to him, even in captivity, he was overwhelmed. Manchan was released from captivity. The marriage was solemnised and the couple left for their own house in Ghatampur.

Narpati had tried to outwardly behave in a very cordial manner with Ranpal and Yasomati, sending presents to them at various functions and other auspicious occasions. Ranpal, being the husband of his step-sister, was considered an important family relation. The enmity was put on the back burner.

One day Ranpal received a letter from Narpati inviting him to Ghatampur for an important family ceremony. The tone of the letter was both inviting and intimidating. It was as if the bravery of Ranpal had been challenged. After reading the letter pregnant Yasomati became nervous. Just then she began sensing several bad omens. She had not paid attention to the daytime howling of jackals, meteor rains during the night and several other happenings usually associated with misfortune befalling some great personality. With the letter from the Ghatma king, she became afraid and tried to dissuade Ranpal from visiting Ghatampur. But Ranpal was determined. He took just one of his trusted personal servants, dressed in the usual battle gear and rode his horse Ranjhampa to Ghatampur.

On arriving at the Ghatmpur fort he was taken inside the palace with great honour and pomp. Inside the fort, he was received by the seven wives of the step-brothers of Yasomati (sisters-in-law of Ranpal) and other womenfolk as per the existing custom in Mithila who were singing traditional welcome folk songs and indulging in jokes with the guest. Princess Vasumati of Bipulgarh, now Queen Vasumati, the youngest sister-in-law, was also present among the women. Ranpal was absorbed in the seemingly warm welcome by the womenfolk. Little did he realise that the Ghatmas had set up several traps to kill him.

As part of his 'test of intelligence' ritual, Ranpal was subjected to a few intriguing situations, each of which could have proved fatal. But he cleverly sidestepped and saved himself with a little help from Vasumati's hints. In the night his only personal servant was quietly abducted and put in prison without anyone's knowledge. In the morning Ranpal was taken to a pond where he was supposed to bathe along with other Ghatma brothers. This was part of an important family ritual where a large number of people from the palace and outside had gathered to witness the event. For this Ranpal had to take out his weapons and clothes including the valuable shield. He entered the pond and was tricked into going to a swimming competition. Little did he know that the Ghatma brothers had hidden daggers in the pond as part of the conspiracy. As soon as he began swimming, all the six brothers pounced on him inside the water and drove daggers into his bare body from all sides. Soon pond water was red with the blood and Ranpal was no more. His body floated on the pond a little later to the astonishment of all the onlookers.

Part-2 : Gugli

Sensing something amiss, Yasomati came running on a palanquin quickly to Ghatampur. But it was too late. Instead of doing something to save her husband, she fell into another trap. She was overpowered and taken to a torture chamber. The Ghatmas wanted to kill her along with the baby which she was carrying inside her womb. Fortunately for her, Queen Vasumati, wife of the youngest brother Sripati, managed to bribe the torturers.

Yasomati was taken to the forest by a couple of *chandals* on the king's orders to be killed and disposed of. Here again, Vasumati managed to bribe the *chandals* handsomely. They took her far away, asked her to change clothes so that they could take her sari and left Yasomati inside a dry well by the side of the road. The *chandals* returned with her sari soaked in some animal blood to be presented to the king as proof of killing.

Yasomati tried to get out of the well but in vain. Late in the evening, Manchan was returning from his business trip and seeing the well asked his servant to fetch water. The servant spotted a woman inside the well and reported to the master. Manchan, with the help of the servant, managed to pull Yasomati out and took her to his house in strict confidence. He spread the news that one of his distant cousins living in a remote village had fallen on hard times and had travelled to Ghatampur to take shelter in his house as she expected a child.

Yasomati was immediately recognised by Manchan's wife. She provided complete confidential care to her as her pregnancy was in a very advanced stage. It was a miracle that even after torture she did not suffer a miscarriage. She gave birth to a boy within a few days. This boy was called Gugli by the masters of the house, a name unsuspecting to outsiders. He was a bright and brave child, just like his father. But he was never told the name of his father.

Gugli (or Gugulia as people began calling him) was known as the nephew of Manchan. As such during his childhood, the boy used to accompany his maternal uncle to the shop or on other errands. When he was five years old, Manchan took him to a distant place to get his education under the care of a Kayasth teacher at Champapur. (See Box for the original narration in Maithili.) He offered the teacher two gold coins and promised to give two donkey loads of gifts when the boy finished his schooling. The teacher had never seen such a generous guardian. He took the boy in his care and began giving him lessons.

दुइ चारि असरफी बनियाँ हरिरा लेल लगाए आबै
माल गुगुलिया भगिनाके कन्हा पर लेल चढ़ाइ आबे
राम राम कए बटिया धएल चम्पापुर के आबै
छन-पहिर मे मामा-भगिना स्कूल पहुँचि गेल आबै

The trader took a few gold coins in his dhoti
Lifted his nephew Gugulia on his shoulders
Praying to God, they took the road to Champapur
Soon both of them arrived at the school

When Gugli grew up to adolescent age and returned from his schooling, he wanted to have a horse to himself for riding. Just around that time, there was a proclamation throughout the Ghatma kingdom about capturing a wild horse which had been roaming around and causing much damage. A few of the palace officials had lost their lives trying to tame and capture that horse. Gugli went in search of that horse who was in reality the son of Ranjhampa, Ranpal's favourite mare left uncared for after his death. The horse was no doubt ferocious but Gugli managed to control him and rein him. As per the terms of the proclamation, the horse now belonged to him.

Around the age of fifteen years, Gugli graduated in all the traditional studies like mathematics, literature, astrology, warfare and social sciences. His teachers proclaimed him one of the finest astrologers and fortune tellers around. His fame spread soon. But people everywhere talked about not knowing the father's name for such a brilliant person. Gugli was hurt and he went to ask his mother. His mother promised to tell him everything only if he kept it confidential till she gave a signal that the opportune moment had arrived. Extracting this promise from Gugli she narrated the entire story of the Ghatma kings and how they murdered his father.

She emphasised that Gugli's maternal uncles, the Ghatma king and his brothers, were his real enemies and he must plan how to take revenge on them. First, he needed to get all the gears of his father kept in Ghatma palace then only he would be safe and secure to execute his plan.

Gugli was now a proud man, the son of a brave father. Just when he was rejoicing in his lineage, Manchan came and informed him that he had been requisitioned by the king for some astrological job. He dressed as a proper astrologer, rode his horse and went to the court. Narpati, his eldest maternal uncle, asked him to check his palm and tell when and how he could annexe Sihulagarh, Vipulgarh and Shovangarh. Gugli looked at the palm, made some observations on the lines and told the king, "O King!, Truth is very bitter, better not be told." Saying this he began withdrawing himself. The king was now more curious to know what the astrologer wanted to tell him. He insisted on listening to whatever good or bad the young astrologer had to tell. Gugli then slowly spoke, "You are a murderer. The sin of murdering the husband of your step-sister is haunting you. You have kept some iron articles of the person you murdered in the palace. These are creating great disturbance for you. The longer you keep them, the more misfortune they will bring. If you want to save yourself, dispose of them quickly. They need to be purified by a tantric." On being asked who that tantric could be, Gugli told him, "If you have faith in me, give them to me. I shall take care of them as per tantric rules."

Soon a servant was sent inside to bring all the stuff which belonged to Ranpal. Those were handed over to Gugli, the Tantric and Astrologer. Gugli collected them and left.

The very next day there was going to be a big assembly of well-known swordsmen from around the country, an event being held in Ghatampur every twelve years. A big arena had been prepared for the purpose outside the palace. People were in a celebratory mood. Suddenly Gugli arrived there fully dressed in his father's battle gear and armed with the special sword.

The first to enter the arena was the dreaded swordsman Bela Nat. He had been unchallenged for many years now. He proudly looked around the crowd and threw his challenge, "Is there anyone who can cross the sword with me?" Complete silence. Suddenly Gugli came out of the crowd and went straight to Bela. Bela saw the youngster and laughed. But Gugli challenged him. A fight ensued. Within minutes Bela realized that the youngster in front of him was far superior and a real swordsman, not easy to handle. He ran away from the arena.

Some whispering took place around the royal seats. King Narpati rose to address the crowd, "The just concluded game was illegal. No one knows the name of the young man's father. The rule of the game does not allow bastards, fallen and persons of unknown roots to take part in this event." Hearing this Gugli roared, "Dear king, keep your ears open and press your breast with both hands because what you are going to hear may lead to a heart attack. Now listen everyone, I am Gugli Ranpal, the proud son of Raiya Arindam Ranpal who was killed by these very people."

The king was shocked but shouted, "Utter lie, unbelievable, we need proof."

Just then Yasomati, riding a horse and dressed in full battle gear, entered the arena and announced, "I am the proof, mother of Gugli. Does anyone have any doubt recognising me?"

Before the royal Ghatma party could react, the entire arena was surrounded by soldiers shouting, "Long Live Gugli Ranpal" and within moments all the six elder Ghatma brothers had been beheaded. The youngest one was not present. It was the wish of Yasomati not to harm him as he was not in any way aligned with his elder brothers and also his wife Vasumati had tried to help save Yasomati.

The control of Ghatampur was taken over by Yasomati and Gugli. The people were assured of peace and prosperity. Gugli had taken revenge for the murder of his father. He later married his maternal sister, the daughter of Vasumati and Sripati.

* * *

IV

Dulra Dayal

[Dulra Dayal is the story of Dayal Singh, a brave sea-farer born in a family of fishermen in the village Bharaura on the bank of old Kamla river in Mithila, and his very devout wife Amaravati (also called Amrautin or Amrouti, a slightly distorted form as sung by many illiterate people) of the same caste whose mother Bahura was a prominent witch of the time in entire Mithila. Bahura lived in Bakhari, a small town in the present-day Begusarai District of Bihar, on the bank of river Tilyuga which joined Kamla and was part of the river trade network through Ganga that operated well beyond the seas, up to Malaysia and Indonesia. She was respectfully referred to as Bahura Thakurain (Thakurain being the feminine of Thakur) because of the enormous power she wielded over river trade passing through Bakhari. Both Bharaura and Bakhari were important river ports where a large number of boats would load and unload their consignments throughout the year.

Dayal Singh was a famous dancer and his tales are also prefixed with the word 'Natua' or 'Natwar', meaning the Dancer. The ballad about Dayal Singh is also available on some YouTube channels under the name of Natua Dayal.

Whereas the course of Kamla river has changed over the hundreds of years to eastward almost a hundred kilometres away, a small rivulet-like lowland exists near Bharaura even today, reminding one that the mighty Kamla once flowed there. While Bharaura does not remember its hero, Dayal Singh, Bakhari is more proud of its witch citizen and people have constructed a temple there remembering Bahura Thakurain.]

Dayal Singh, affectionately called Dulra Dayal (*Dulra* is an affectionate address) by the village folk, was the son of a rich fisherman trader Bishambhar Sahni, also known as the king of Bharaura, and his extremely devout wife Gajmoti. The entire Bharaura village and also others nearby worshipped river Kamla, referring to her as the Goddess Mother Kamleswary, as the river was the lifeline for the entire region, particularly for fishermen. Kamleswary was considered to be an incarnation of Goddess Laxmi. There was a Kamla Mandap, a special temple, for the worship of Kamla in the village. Every year during Aswin Purnima (full moon day in Aswin, sometime in the month of October) there used to be elaborate celebrations for the Kamla worship where in addition to the villagers of Bharaura, people from adjoining areas and even some faraway places used to take part.

Bishambhar Sahni had a younger brother, Bhimal, who was unmarried and showered all his love and affection on Dayal like his own son. Bhimal was a famous wrestler and a fearless seafarer. He also performed the duty of military commander for his elder brother's kingdom. After the unfortunate death of Bishambhar Sahni in a boat accident during a fishing expedition, he became the de facto guardian of Dayal Singh.

From early childhood, Dayal Singh showed great interest in sailing and dancing. He was also a committed devotee of Kamleswary (the Goddess form of river Kamla revered and worshipped throughout Mithila). Worshipping Kamla daily was his routine. He was getting trained by his Guru Mangal, an old man of the same village, who had been a very successful seafarer in his heydays and also possessed a large bunch of very intelligent crows. These crows were a great companion and guide to Mangal during long voyages. They would sense danger and warn him. Dayal Singh was very interested in listening to tales of seafarers passing through the port of Bharaura and would always run to such people to listen to their experiences. By the time Dayal Singh turned eighteen, he possessed exceptional knowledge about the river currents, weather, cloud formation, rain, storms, river animals etc. He had also mastered several dance forms. His fame both as a dancer and water astrologer spread far and wide. With the help of his guru Mangal, Dayal Singh had also learnt to interpret the signals given by crows during the voyage.

Bahura Thakurain controlled the important port of Bakhari which was the main transit route from the port of Bharaura on the Kamla river to river Ganga and further onward to the sea. Because of her mastery over witchcraft, she began considering herself a Goddess and told the local villagers to worship her instead of worshipping Kamla or Kamleswary. Fearing the wrath of Bahura, the locals grudgingly accepted her command.

On the occasion of Durga Puja Dayal Singh was scheduled to perform his dance in front of the temple of Kamla on the night of Ashtami, the eighth day of the Puja. This annual affair attracted large crowds of people from both near and distant villages. People gathered to watch the magnificent dance performance of Dayal Singh. During his eighteenth year, Dayal Singh performed an unforgettable dance sequence. During that night after the conclusion of his dance, a twelve-year-old beautiful maid named Amaravati, daughter of Bahura Thakurain of Bakhari, came forward to present the first offerings to Kamla Devi. Dayal Singh and Amaravati's eyes met each other and instantly they fell in love. The families decided to solemnize the marriage even though Bhimal Sahni was apprehensive of Bahura's inimical designs and her boastful ways of seeking people's worship.

A large contingent of seven hundred men started from Bharaura in the marriage party, led by Bhimal Sahni, with the groom Dayal Singh seated on a decorated red palanquin. Bhimal had warned the men in the marriage party about unnatural happenings which Bahura Thakurain might display as part of her boasting about magic and witchcraft. The contingent travelled in several large boats. On their arrival at Bakhari, the marriage party was taken to the outer courtyard in Bahura's palace and well received according to the local tradition. When the time came for the invocation of the local family deity, Bahura sent words to Bhimal that in Bakhari, she was the Goddess and people treated her as the local deity. But Bhimal refused to worship her. Instead, he followed the traditional worship of Mother Kamla. This enraged Bahura but she did not object immediately. She decided to take revenge at an opportune moment.

The marriage rituals commenced in full jubilation. The womenfolk began singing auspicious marriage songs and the Brahmans began chanting Veda hymns. The groom was taken to the inner courtyard surrounded by a large retinue of young women. After the traditional welcoming ritual of '*parichhan*' for the groom, the other marriage rituals were performed one after another as per the local custom and finally the groom applied the traditional vermillion on the line made by parting hair on the bride's forehead and then took seven rounds around the fire chanting the vow of living together in all good and bad circumstances.

In the meantime, preparations began for feeding the marriage party. Seats were spread on the ground and the entire marriage party was invited for the gala dinner. It was now time for Bahura to show her magical powers to them. When the men were seated on the mats, they could not believe their eyes finding themselves all sitting on the back of large tortoises. Everyone was terrified and wanted to run away. Bhimal however calmed them telling them about Bahura's cleverness. Soon banana leaves started falling from above in front of each person and similarly, food items also were thrown from above, though apparently no one could be seen doing the acts. More surprises lay in store for the marriage party. When they commenced eating they found sand in their mouth although the food on the banana leaves looked fresh, delectable and cooked well. The marriage party was losing patience and getting more and more terrified. No one knew Bahaura's designs.

All of a sudden, fire arrows came flying from above and burning the men. Bhimal told his men to chant Kamla's prayers and run away. They did as advised. Before he could react, he saw someone rushing from the inner courtyard towards him. The person was a young lady, Phoolmati, sister-in-law of Amaravati (wife of her brother), who had rushed to inform Bhimal that Dayal Singh's life was in danger. With a quick reflex of mind, he rushed to the inner courtyard, lifted Dayal Singh and began running as fast as he could. (See Box for the original narration in Maithili.)

ई बतिया सुनि कए फुलमतिया कें माया गेलै जे आब
ओ दौड़ि कएॅ सब बात भीमल कें कहिये देलक जे आब
जान बचा कए अपन गाम लौट न जाउ आब
नहि तऽ तोहर भतीजा के जान न बचतौ आब
ई सुनि भीमल सहनी भतीजा के लए भागि गेल जे आब
अइ बात के पता बहुरा के झट दए लागि गेल जे आब

Hearing this Phoolmatia felt pity
She ran and told everything to Bhimal Sahni
Take your nephew and run for life
Otherwise your nephew will lose his life
Bhimal Sahni took Dulra and quickly ran away
Bahura learnt about this immediately after

Bahura saw her designs of taking revenge on Bhimal not materialising. She immediately called her witch disciples and asked them to throw fire arrows towards the running marriage party of Bharaura. They tried their best but as the entire party was singing prayers in praise of Mother Kamla, they found an invisible shield protecting them as they moved along. The witches became helpless.

Bahura herself began following them and shouted to Bhimal to look back. Bhimal did not pay any heed and kept running. But when he was about to reach Rosera, as ill luck would have it, he momentarily looked back. Just then a fire-arrow hit his left eye and he lost that eye. Somehow he along with all others reached

Bharaura safely.

Dulra Dayal was left brooding over the entire sequence of events. His dream of consummating the marriage with his young bride remained unfulfilled. In Bakhari, Amaravati was also in tears having missed the opportunity of spending time with her husband. Dayal Singh took a bold, revolutionary and unconventional decision: to take revenge on the people of Bakhari, not with the help of an army but with the use of dance in its purest form so as to make them surrender to Mother Kamla. He also needed to be as knowledgeable as his mother-in-law in the art of witchcraft and sorcery in order to show her down.

Thus began his long voyage to various parts of the country in search of teachers for special dances. His Guru Mangal had given him some leads in this connection. He was to learn the *Khatachakra Nr̩tya* (six-cycle dance) from the revered Kama Yogini at Kamrup-Kamakhya. He was to observe strict celibacy, never to look at the Yogini's upper body as during the dance she would sometimes get stark-naked also, and no matter how inviting or pressured by any young woman, never enter into a sexual relationship.

Kamrup-Kamakhya, in present-day Assam, was known to be an epicentre of training in sorcery, witchcraft and all kinds of black magic. The place was also famous for the metamorphosis of humans: witches used to convert strong young men into various animals like rams, tigers and even birds during the daytime. They would again change them to humans during the night when they needed to satisfy their sexual urges. Such stories floated in the countryside of Mithila for a long time.

Dayal Singh travelled to Kamrup-Kamakhya in a specially constructed boat. But a long journey had cast its shadow on the health of the young man. He went near a pond and being tired and hungry, went into the pond and began drinking water. When he lifted his face he was startled to find seven hundred handsome young women, all stark-naked, laughing and chatting in the pond. All of them fell for the young strong Dayal Singh and wanted to marry him. He was caught by the young female army and brought to their Guru, an elderly lady Yashodha, who was well-known for her deep knowledge of witchcraft, sorcery and black magic. Dayal Singh pleaded with the elderly lady to accept him as a disciple and teach him all that she knew. He told her to treat him as her son as he accepted her as a mother in that remote place. Dayal's entreating was so strong and pleasing that Yashodha could not deny his requests. She directed her seven hundred disciples to teach every little detail of the art in full glory. It took six months for Dayal Singh to master all the tricks of the trade. Now he was confident enough to beat his mother-in-law Bahura in the art of witchcraft.

Dayal Singh recalled his Guru's instructions to find Kama Yogini in Kamakhya temple on a new moon night where in the darkness of the night a larger number of yoginis would come to dance there. Dayal was to play *Mridangam* when the traditional players would get exhausted and fall to the ground. He went to the temple on the next new moon night and managed to attract the attention of Kama Yogini by his expert playing of *Mridangam* in the night. He begged Kama to teach him the *Khatachakra Nr.tya*. After much persuasion, Kama agreed but Dayal Singh had to pay a heavy price. Kama would also not let Dayal Singh become free. Most of the time he would be kept transformed as a ram.

One night Kama saw a bright light approaching from the sky into her chamber where Dayal Singh was kept as a ram. The light transformed itself into Amaravati. With her power of virtuosity and the blessings of Goddess Kamla, she had come to know about the condition of her husband under Kama's care. With Kamla's blessings, she was transformed into a streak of light and reached the quarters of Kama Yogini at Kamrup-Kamakhya instantly. She transformed Dayal Singh into a human being in the presence of Kama. She told her that no power would be able to transform Dayal Singh back to any animal form henceforth. Kama realised her folly and saluted Amaravati. Dayal Singh and Amaravati together went to the Kamakhya temple, offered prayers by dancing together and then Amaravati vanished as a streak of light in the sky.

Kama would frequently get naked during the dance practice sessions. But Dayal Singh always remembered his Guru's words and would never look up towards her body. He would always concentrate on following her foot movements and be glued to the feet. Kama was surprised and annoyed at such behaviour. She tried many tricks to get physical with Dayal Singh but did not succeed. As the days passed, she was pleasantly surprised at the progress of Dayal Singh's dance lessons.

After a few months, when Dayal Singh had mastered four of the six-cycle dance, Kama told him that he would now have to go to Shankhagram situated at the confluence of river Ganga and the ocean, what is present-day Gangasagar Island. The only person knowing the last two sequences of the dance was Bhuvan Mohini, princess of Shankhagram. Dayal Singh paid his respects to Kama Yogini and took her leave to commence the next journey to Sankhagram.

During such a long absence of Dayal Singh from Mithila, a villainous character, Jai Singh, who wanted to marry Amaravati, and had gained the confidence of Bahura Thakurain through his treacherous moves, took the help of some unscrupulous elements in the Nepal mountains and tried to bend the water flow of Kamla by putting large boulders in water near Bhima where the river was very narrow. Kamla no longer flew south into Mithila. The entire riverbed downstream became dry within no time. The port at Bharaura became dry and no longer navigable. This pleased Bahura as the power of Kamla as a route for the river trade was now extinct. She hoped that over time people would forget worshipping Kamla and she could become the reining deity for local worship.

Dayal Singh arrived at Shankhagram and presented himself to the court of Princess Bhuvan Mohini. He narrated what dance he had learnt so far and expressed his desire to learn the remaining sequences of the six-cycle dance. Bhuvan Mohini first wanted to see what Dayal Singh had learnt. The opportunity arrived on the occasion of the monthly worship of the reigning deity of the Bay of Bengal, Bangeswari. On the last day of the three-day event, Dayal

Singh was called to dance in front of a large audience. His performance exceeded all expectations of everyone there and he was crowned the star Dancer of that year. He was allowed unhindered access to the court and meet with the Princess. She agreed to give him the necessary lessons.

Dayal Singh's stay at Shankhagram was much longer than he desired. This was particularly because of two reasons – the Queen Mother wanted him to marry Bhuvan Mohini and also the princess herself kept delaying the dance instructions to have his company longer. Even though Dayal Singh very politely declined the offer of marriage, he was appointed the chief of the Shankhagram's flotilla and was requested to go on a voyage and trade their wares as the old chief had died. Dayal Singh also earned a lot of money in the trade. Finally, the princess gave him the last set of dance instructions. During his rather long stay at Shankhagram, he met several people, important among them being the trader Vijay Malla from Mithila. Both had known each other because of being connected to the same trade. After completing his dance lessons Dayal Singh managed to plan his return with the flotilla of Vijaya Malla, which had very experienced brothers Gahar Malla and Gohil Malla as sailor chiefs.

Dayal Singh had by now attained the fame of a dancer par excellence who could heal anyone's physical and mental ailments using the power of his dance. The dance symbolized Lord Shiva Himself and it was the power of Shiva which helped in healing. On the way, he cured the wife of King Haans Datta of Assam who had been suffering from an incurable disease. In return, Haans Datta sent a large contingent of his military with Dayal Singh to protect him on his return journey. Dayal Singh's power of dance made him immune to attacks by witches. He was also being protected by Goddess Kamleswary who travelled with the flotilla as a bird providing an invisible shield for Dayal Singh.

"Dulra Dayal is coming home, laden with riches in a big flotilla. He has mastered all the arts in Kamrup-Kamakhya. He is protected by Goddess Kamleswary and no witch on this earth can harm him now. He is unconquerable." – the news travelled faster than the flotilla itself moved. His attainment about dance and witchcraft was being amplified by the villagers en route and transmitted to wider areas. The news reached the ears of Bahura Thakurain at Bakhari too. She became restless. She feared retribution from Bhimal Sahni, uncle of Dayal Singh for her acts during the marriage of Dayal Singh. She tried to damage the flotilla and stop its progress further inward. She sent words to her disciple and accomplished witch Asini, also a prostitute, having a base at Manihari Ghat. But Gohil Malla himself guarded the flotilla and forbade all the men from disembarking and visiting any prostitute there. Asini could not do any harm to anyone. Bahura tried many tricks available in her store of witchcraft, like sending epidemic fever using birds to the flotilla, throwing all sorts of remotely controlled fatal weapons and fire engulfing arrows, attempting to poison food and drinking water but all her attempts were in vain, the weapons were either destroyed or their effects nullified well before arriving near the flotilla of Vijay Malla. Wary of Bahura's designs, the flotilla did not stop at Bakhari but proceeded further onward to take a break at Rosera Ghat, another important port town. Bahura felt devastated and defeated for the first time in her life.

Jay Singh came to know about Bahura's failed attempts and decided to do something himself. He wss still hopeful to turn the table on Dayal Singh, please Bahura and in return marry Amaravati. He sought the help of the king of Rosera, himself a villainous character and the two together devised a plan to entrap Dayal Singh. Little did they realise that Dayal Singh had attained enormous power through his dance and it would be very difficult to inflict any physical harm to him. Even though Dayal Singh was taken in captivity by tricking him into accepting the invitation for a Kamla Puja by the king of Rosera, it was the king who suffered, getting inflicted with a severe stomach ailment which could not be cured by his court physicians. Finally, he could only be cured by Dayal Singh's intervention. The king of Rosera became a great admirer of Dayal Singh. Thus came an end to Jai Singh's designs.

At Rosera Vijay Malla interacted with many seafarers and got the news about the river Kamla in Bharaura becoming dry. They explained to him that the old port in River Kamla had dried up and become inoperative. However, Bhimal Sahni and the villagers had found the nearby Bagmati River as an alternative location to establish a port infrastructure. Bagmati was flowing some four to five kilometres away and was not as convenient as Kamla for the people of Bharaura but that was the best option in the given circumstances. Vijaya Malla was advised to proceed and take his flotilla into Bagmati.

Amaravati came to know that Dayal Singh had passed by Bakhari but did not stop there. She was aggrieved that he did not even send any word to her through any messenger. She knew that her mother had been acting against her wishes and had planned to harm Dayal Singh and his entourage in every possible way. She was greatly upset and sent a messenger to meet Dayal Singh at Rosera. The messenger carried the words which implied that Amaravati begged for forgiveness for her mother. Dayal Singh was very pleased to receive the messenger and assured Amaravati through the messenger that he had to skip Bakhari in the larger interest of the accompanying flotilla and its sailors. He further assured that whatever he had learned during his visits to Kamrup-Kamakhya and elsewhere was always going to be used for the betterment of humankind and never used to harm anyone, the least of all his mother-in-law. Amaravati's mother was also very much like his own mother. No matter what his mother-in-law thought or did, he always would treat her with the utmost reverence like his own mother.

The flotilla sailed further and arrived through the newly constructed port in river Bagmati close to Dulara's village. People became busy disembarking and unloading the boats. The goods and riches were being carried from the port to the village on bullock carts.

Dayal Singh saw the dry bed of Kamla River and was crestfallen. He could not fathom what had happened to the river and which of his enemies had blocked the flow and where. He had always faithfully worshipped Mother Kamla. Then why did she become cross with the entire population of the Mithila region?

He quickly gathered some of the villagers and told them to dig the dry river bed as deep as they could and make the embankments stronger. Without losing time, he took a couple of strong-bodied aides and set out northward to investigate and make amends to restore the flow of the river. Kilometre after kilometre, as he traversed numerous villages and talked to the local people, he heard the same sad tale, dry river bed and little irrigation, famine-like conditions with crops failing. In every village, he requested the villagers to use the opportunity of the river being dry to dig deeper and also make the embankments stronger. He assured them that he was on the mission to bring Kamla back to Mithila and no matter how much time it might take, he was sure that he would succeed. He distributed some money also among the needy villagers.

Finally, towards the end of his journey, he entered what is present-day Nepal's Sindhuli district and went further up the mountain towards the source of the river. Very close to the river's origin, he was dismayed to find that large boulders had been placed at a location where the width of the river was narrow. The boulders had blocked the flow of the river southward and the accumulated water had formed a huge lake there. That was the reason for the river becoming dry downstream. The locals did not know who had placed the boulders and they had been not much concerned as they got water from the overflowed lake. They had not cared to investigate the source of water and whether the river flowed further south down or not.

Dulra quickly got to the business. With some effort by the locals and his men, he managed to remove the boulders one by one. Soon the flow resumed. After making sure that no one again dared to block the path of water flow at that constricted location, he returned southward. He was pleasantly surprised to find that the water had kept moving down south and preceded his path. Soon all along the way the river was full of water and it had also flooded nearby regions, filling the parched ponds and lakes. By the time he reached his village, people were rejoicing at the return of water in the river. Dulra was hailed as the second Bhagirath (the first refers to the legendary king of Ikshvaku dynasty, who brought the River Ganga from Heaven onto the Earth) for having brought Kamla back to Mithila.

Dulra's Guru Mangal called an assembly of the villagers and set the tone for the week-long worship of Mother Kamla in full glory as in the olden days. Dulra himself would be the chief worshipper and dancer for the entire duration. A day was settled and preparations began. This time the celebration was financed by Vijay Malla and Gohil Malla brothers who had accompanied Dulra from the sea.

The Kamla worship and dance celebrations were held for one full week and kept the people busy. The entire region rejoiced over the event. The port at Bharaura was again bustling and the sailors began their businesses. When the dust settled over the celebrations, Dulra decided to begin preparations for his proposed *Dwiragaman* trip to Bakhari to bring his wife.

The villagers who had been part of the marriage party of Dayal Singh on the first occasion had not forgotten the horrific treatment they had received by the witch queen Bahura Thakurain, mother-in-law of Dulra. No one wanted a repeat of those experiences and hence the villagers showed their disinclination to join the party again to Bakhari. Dayal Singh however made a different set of arrangements for the party and assured everyone that no harm would come to anyone till he would be with them. It was decided to take their own ration and not go close to Bakhari within the region of influence of Bahura Thakurain. They would always stay put in their boats and would be guarded by able men.

The party began the journey towards Bakhari. It was necessary to send words to Bahura Thakurain as the trip involved a major event in her family – *Dwiragaman*, which meant that her daughter and wife of Dayal Singh would be going to her in-laws. This was a very important occasion for every married girl in Mithila.

Bahura was not to stay calm on such an occasion. She had not forgotten how Bhimal had snatched Dayal Singh from her clutches during the marriage and ran away safely, albeit losing one of his eyes in the process. She was also aware that despite her best efforts to keep Kamla away, Dayal Singh had managed to bring the river back. She was afraid that her determination to abolish Kamla worship and establish herself as the reigning queen goddess of waterways would not be fruitful anymore. So she decided to act firmly. She called all her disciples and instructed them to employ all their knowledge and tricks of witchcraft to frighten the marriage party accompanying Dulra and force them to return or else perish.

The flotilla carrying the marriage party proceeded smoothly. Suddenly people saw a dark cloud approaching them with ferocity as if it would rain and submerge the entire flotilla. The cloud consisted of bees. Dulra began Kamla's prayers on his boat. To everyone's dismay the entire sky was filled with *Neelkanth* (the Indian Roller) birds and the bees disappeared from the scene altogether. People heaved a sigh of relief.

After some time when evening approached, the flotilla came to a halt near a reasonably clean part of the river bank. Preparations began for cooking the evening meal. When it was just the time for setting the dinner, again something unexplained happened. From nowhere, a large number of jackals came to the bank and began howling and creating ferocious scenes, trying to jump onto the boats and spoil the food. The number of jackals was so large that people on the boats were not capable of controlling them individually by any means. Dulra called one of his aides, and instructed him to sprinkle the treated water from Kamla kept in a special pot. As soon as water fell on his body, he was transformed into a huge royal Bengal tiger. The tiger jumped upon the jackals which fled immediately. Dulra came back to human shape again after getting sprinkled with the same water. Thus their food was saved and also had a peaceful night.

Dulra told the accompanying entourage that these were just Bahura Takhurain frightening them using her tricks of witchcraft.

He also warned them that more such wonders would follow to scare them away. True to his prediction and others' apprehensions, the next morning they saw bundles of uprooted trees flying through the air towards their boats. In addition, Bahura had instructed her disciples to use the tricks of witchcraft to fill all the drinking water wells with worms except the one close to her own house.

With his presence of mind, always chanting prayers of River Kamla or Mother Kamlewary, Dulra was able to drive away the dangers close to his boats. But his main purpose, to get a formal welcome into the Thakurain household for the purpose of *Dwiragaman* was still not in sight. He decided to go all alone, with just one aide carrying seven hundred silk saris and accompanying dresses and ornaments. He knew that Thakurain had well-trained seven hundred female witches, whom she would surely deploy to trouble him. The aide also carried gifts for Dulra's wife, mother-in-law and other family members as per the existing tradition.

Dulra straightway went to the only well where worms were not there in the water. He began his dance impromptu. Soon, as he had guessed, all the seven hundred witches accompanied by their seven hundred phantomised spirits came there and began hurling fire arrows at Dulra. To their surprise, the fire arrows turned into flowers of various kinds before falling on Dulra's body and they spread a mix of fragrances around. To teach the witches a lesson, Dulra himself began a fire dance. The result was fire spreading all around, all the witches caught in that fire. Their saris were burnt and they had to throw them away, becoming naked in the process. They ran helter-skelter to save themselves. Showing his magnanimity, Dulra stopped the fire dance, called the witches near and told them of his purpose of visit. He gave them the silk saris to change and asked them to go back and make preparations for the formal welcome ritual '*Parichhan*' being accorded to any son-in-law arriving for the *Dwiragaman.*

The seven hundred witches, now scared of the power of Dulra's dance, went back and began preparations for '*Parichhan*' against the wishes of Bahura. With Amaravati's sister-in-law Phoolmati in the lead, they walked singing traditional folk songs to welcome Dulra formally. He was brought to the inner quarters and given ceremonial food.

Bahura was still not able to come to terms with her ego. Her every plan to harm Dulra was going empty, in addition, her own people were being hurt and subjected to humiliation so that finally they would take sides with Dulra. She was not going to give up so easily. She went into her prayer room and prayed to the family deity. When he appeared as a dark cloud, she narrated her woos and asked for guidance to save her ego. The deity tried to reason with her that her days to use witchcraft to harm people had passed and now it was the positivity of Dulra's dance that was becoming superior as it had the power to heal. Even then just to keep her happy, he gave her a hint to try if she could enter Dulra's bed chamber and take away his life through the nose.

This was the last attempt that Bahura made. Knowing fully well that it was against all nicety and tradition to enter the bed chamber where her daughter and son-in-law were sleeping, she stealthily entered the room and proceeded towards Dulra. Suddenly Amaravati was woken and so was Dulra. Both of them began the prayer dance of Kamleswary which incensed Bahura. To counter the effect she threw a powerful fire arrow towards Dulra but to her surprise, it boomeranged and hit her causing her sari to catch fire. She was saved by the quick intervention of Dulra still praying to Mother Kamleswary. Bahura had been defeated. She realised her folly at the end. She gave up her bad thoughts and doings and agreed to the worship of river Kamla as Mother Kamleswary.

The next morning the entire village was summoned and requested to prepare for a grand Kamla worship. Bahura then sent a request to Bhimal to come to her residence with the entire party and oblige her by taking food there. When Bhimal arrived and met Bahura, she sprung a surprise. She opened the knot of her sari where a snail shell had been kept. Bhimal's eye, which Bahura had extracted by her witchcraft, had been kept neatly within the shell. She took that out and stuck it into the hollow of Bhimal's forehead.

Within no time, he began seeing with both his eyes. The entire marriage party was very happy now that Bahura had given up the path of enmity and destruction and taken up good work.

In the evening as per tradition, Amaravati was given a touching send-off by the people of the entire Bakhari village to her husband's village. She boarded the decorated boat with Dulra and the party departed.

On reaching Bharaura, the bride was given a warm and ceremonial welcome by the entire village. Dulra's mother Gajmoti's joys knew no bounds. The welcome was followed by Kamla worship and then a set of dances by Dulra. He was now a folk hero and unquestioned dancer par excellence in the entire Mithila.

* * *

V
Luvhari-Kushahari

[The story of Luv and Kush, the twin sons of Lord Ram and Sita, is known from many sources including the Ramyana. But the ballad version propagating in Mithila is somewhat different.]

Lord Ram had returned to Ayodhya along with his wife Sita and brother Laxman and the entourage consisting of a large contingent of the monkey army which was led by Hanuman. They had been given a royal reception by Mother Koshalya and others including the people of Ayodhya. It was time to take some rest after the strenuous fourteen years of forest dwelling.

Sita, already in an advanced stage of pregnancy, was taking rest in her chamber. She was surrounded by several women, her sisters (wives of the other three brothers of Ram) and some sisters-in-law (cousins of Ram). Everyone was in a gay mood, playing jokes and jest and laughing at each other. One of the sisters-in-law, Kulamati, just asked Sita to make a sketch of Ravana. Sita pleaded her inability saying she had never seen the face of the Lanka King, not even his feet. She had always been looking at Mother Earth whenever the Lanka King used to come to Ashok Vatika. In spite of her denials, many women began requesting. Finally, Sita drew some sketches from whatever she had heard in Lanka about Ravan. By ill luck the top part of Sita's little finger touched the mouth of the sketch. The little finger was known to contain Amrit, the nectar of immortality.

Immediately the sketch came to life and Ravan stood in front of everyone in the chamber. The demon began his tantrums and terrified all. All the women were frightened and ran away from there. Finally, Hanuman was sent to capture the demon in Sita's chamber and punish him. He also did not succeed. But by some miracle, the demon itself was brought down as the effect of Amrit had expired, the whole thing being a transient phenomenon.

झूठि फूसि हनुमान बजै छथि दगा करै छथि आब यौ
जै जंगल मे कोनो फल नै हनुमान के दियौ बनिसार यौ
अन्न फल बिनु हनुमान मारल जेता आब यौ
सिरी जानकी के लँएके जड़ियौ रिखिया जंगल आब यौ
पाँच हाथ के झोपड़ी बना कए दिऔन आब बनिसार यौ
एहन कलंकी तिरियो के हम ने देखs चाहै छी आब यौ
गरा पकड़ि कए जंगल मे बनबास दियौ आब यौ
जे जंगल माहुर जंगल छल ताहि मे देल बनिसार यौ

Hanuman is telling lies and is cheating now
Send him to the jungle where there are no fruits
Hanuman will die for want of grains and fruits
Take Sri Janki to Rikhia forest now
Make seven feet long hut and banish her there
I don't want to see such a slanderous woman
Hold her by the neck and banish her to a jungle
She was banished to a jungle having only poisonous fruits

The event passed but there was uproar in the town. People began discussing whether Sita had really never seen Ravan or had ever taken a glance at him. Lord Ram was scared of the scandalous nature of the event and people's reactions. This led him to make a harsh decision. He asked Laxman to take Sita to a forest where there would be only trees of poisonous fruits. Even Hanuman was not spared. His fault was not providing a truthful description of the demonic nature of Ravan. So Ram told Laxman to send Hanuman to a distant forest having no fruit trees.

Laxman, always truthful to his elder brother's wishes and orders, obeyed. He took Sita to a distant forest where there were only trees of poisonous fruits. Then he took Hanuman to another distant forest where no fruit trees ever grew. While he carried out the orders, he was also torn within himself of the conscious fact that not only Sita was pregnant, but she was a very dear sister-in-law and mother-like to him. Similarly for Hanuman, he was filled with remorse while taking him to a fruitless forest. Hanuman had been his saviour during the Lanka war. Without Hanuman's heroic effort in bringing the *Sanjivani* herb, Laxman would have surely died. But the orders of the King had to be given preference over all other human emotions. Laxman began weeping.

The news of Sita being banished to a forest amid her advanced stage of pregnancy caused uproar in heaven as well. All the fifty-six crores gods became afraid of some impending disaster. Sita was known for her virtuous nature and to cast aspersions on her character was to cast doubt on the warmth of sunrays. Eventually, all the gods decided to remain alert and protect Sita. By the wishes of gods, several sages descended on the forest where Sita had been banished and began living at some distance by constructing suitable huts for them. Sage Vashisht, the Guru of Lord Ram, was also among them. Vashisht had his ashram close to that of Sita and he always kept an eye on her without directly talking to her.

Sita was managing her life with the help of whatever edible roots she could dig, as the forest had no edible fruits. She had no one to complain to except her fate. Three months into her banishment, she gave birth to a son. This child was called *Luvhari* (or Luv in short). Just after birth, the child began jumping high in the sky. He would thump his chest and thighs as if challenging someone in a wrestling bout. His thumping of thighs was so violent that it shook the throne of King Ram in Ayodhya. The shaking became frequent because of the frequent thumping of thighs by the newborn Luvhari, it was also sometimes accompanied by an earthquake and a fire in some parts of Ayodhya. Lord Ram could not understand the origin of these sudden happenings without any provocation from his side. He was very surprised as well as worried. He then called an assembly of sages, pandits and astrologers to his court and asked them to decipher the reason for the shaking of the throne and the sudden occurrence of earthquake and fire.

After long deliberations, the learned men unanimously declared, "A superior brave person has been born on this earth, who will someday defeat Ram in battle and rule over Ayodhya." Lord Ram was now more worried after hearing this forecast by the pandits. But there was nothing he could do. The pandits had no suggestions to avoid this calamity. It was written in the fate of Lord Ram, there was no deterrence for that.

The gods in heaven were overjoyed at the birth of Luvhari. They became more vigilant now to protect not only Sita but the newborn as well. Lord Shiva, Vishwakarma and Bhairav in particular took special care that no harm should ever come to the child. On the ninth day after the birth of the child, Sita went to take a bath in the river Ganga as part of the ritual to cleanse herself. She left Luvhari unattended and alone in the hut. While taking a bath in the river she noticed a mother monkey with her child clinging to her body and jumping from one tree to another. She thought for a moment and then told the mother monkey, "What a fool you are! Don't you ever dread that if the child loses grip, she will fall to the ground or in the river and you will not get a trace of its body." The mother monkey replied, "Why are you worried about my child? Don't you dread what will happen to your own child whom you left alone in that hut in the forest? Did you ever think that some wild animal could come and lift the child and go away? What will you get then?"

Sita was alarmed. It had suddenly dawned on her that she committed a grave mistake by leaving her newborn unattended. She ran from there.

In the meantime, when Sage Vashisht saw Sita going away to take a bath, he came and took the newborn to his hut to keep him protected from any harm by wild animals. Lord Shiva also wanted to go and protect the child in the absence of his mother. He came to the hut and found it empty. He had no idea that the child had been taken by Sage Vashisht. He got worried about not finding the child there. He thought that surely some wild animal had come and taken the child away. Fearing the wrath of Sita, he quickly made a child using *Kush* (a somewhat taller grass considered sacred and used in all the Yajnas) and brought that to life with his special powers. When Sita returned, she found the child and was happy. She immediately began nursing the child little realising what had happened in the intervening period. However, seeing Sita returning from the river, Vashisht also came to the hut carrying the newborn in his arms. Both Sita and Vashisht looked at each other in amazement. There were two identical babies now. Soon the riddle was solved by Lord Shiva himself. Sita took both the babies. The one made from Kush was called *Kushahari* (or Kush in short). She gave equal attention to both the babies. Kush was as brave as his elder sibling Luv. He also began jumping sky-high and thumping his chest and thighs, each time causing earthquakes in Ayodhya and shaking the throne of Lord Ram. The wild animals of the forest were now terrified because of the divine powers of the two brothers.

When Luv and Kush attained the age of six years, they sought a blessing from their mother to go hunting in the deep forest. But Mother Sita would not permit it as the entire jungle belonged to Lord Ram's kingdom. After much entreating by the two young lads, she agreed. They touched the feet of their mother to get blessed and they went to the jungle for hunting. They hunted countless lions and tigers, not to mention smaller animals like deer, boar, bear and antelopes. They also managed to kill a few of the Rakshasas and Rakshasis. They wanted to go further on to Uttarakhand but Mother Sita strictly forbade them from going there. She knew that the horse of Ashwamedh Yajna was kept roaming in Uttarakhand. The two brothers did not ask their mother and quietly went towards Uttarakhand. Hunting and travelling they went to the place where the horse Balikaran was roaming. It was said that no one had been born who could catch the reigns of that horse. The horse was supposedly untamed. But the two brothers slowly walked towards the horse and began caressing him, touching his mane and simply massaging his body. The horse enjoyed caressing and did not harm the two young lads. He became friendly towards them and asked who they were. The young lads said that they were the sons of Mother Sita. Hearing the name of Sita, the horse began weeping. He recalled his earlier days spent with Mother Sita. He had been always grateful to her for the care she gave him. He asked the lads if they could take him to Mother Sita for a *Darshan* (getting a glimpse). But the boys did not know how to take the horse with them. Then Balikaran himself suggested that both of them together ride on his back and he would walk to their hut where Mother Sita should be found. He lowered his body so that the young boys could easily mount on the back. When they were comfortably seated, the horse started trotting slowly, taking care that his riders were not put to the slightest inconvenience.

After arriving at the hut of Mother Sita, Balikaran lowered his body and the two boys alighted. Then he went and touched the feet of the Mother and began wallowing there. Sita blessed the horse and caressed him. Luvhari and Kushahari left the horse there and went back to the forest for hunting.

The horseman found the horse missing and went in search of the animal. On the way, he met Luvhari and Kushahari. While talking to them he learnt that they had taken the horse to Mother Sita. He was infuriated at this audacious behaviour of the two brothers and challenged them saying, "If you consider yourself brave and strong, go to Kamldah. There is a special five-faced lotus flowering in that lake. Pluck that flower and bring that to me."

Such a challenge was almost like an insult for Luvhari and Kushahari. They considered it an affront to their bravery and strength. Both of them went back to their mother and asked for permission as well as blessings to go to Kamaldah Lake and pluck the five-faced lotus. Sita agreed and blessed them, "Your body will become indestructible; you will not be harmed by anyone or anything, no matter what the attempt might be."

Having thus been blessed by their mother, the two brothers set out for Kamaldah Lake. They were walking briskly because of excitement to reach there at the earliest. Soon they arrived at the lake. They were tired because of the long journey. They sat down under the shade of a *pakar* tree on the bank of the lake. There was a cool breeze blowing and soon Kushahari found himself dosing. His brother advised him to make himself comfortable and sleep for some time. Kushahari went into deep slumber. He slept for seven days and seven nights at a stretch.

In the meantime Luvharidecided to get into the lake and pluck the five-faced lotuses which were there in plenty. He was astonished to find that each such lotus was guarded by two poisonous snakes. The leader of the snakes was one Bachharnag. Because poison was frequently released by those snakes into the lake water, that water had also turned poisonous. Nevertheless, Luvhari entered the lake and proceeded towards a lotus flower. Suddenly the snakes guarding them attacked him in unison. He stayed cool, played his flute and called Garud. Hearing the sound of Luvhari's flute, Garud came there along with his clan and devoured all the snakes. The leader Bachharnag was however saved as he hid himself. But he was in no position to harm Luvhari now. While going back Garud and his fellow birds flipped their wings so violently that a wave was created in the lake cleansing it of all the poisonous effects. Its water became crystal clear and sweet. Luvhari then caught Bachharnag, tied his mouth with a grass string and threw him on the ground where he became immobile.

Lord Ram came to know that someone had ransacked Kamaldah Lake. He became very angry, called his nephews, Kulamati's sons Sal and Vishal and ordered them to go and catch whosoever had harmed Kamaldah. When Sal and Vishal arrived at the lake they found Luvhari alone. They started jumping in anger and challenged him to a fight. For some time they were engaged in only verbal duels but soon fights came to body blows, wrestling manoeuvres and hand-to-hand grappling. The fighting continued for seven days and seven nights. All along Kushahari was in deep slumber. The brothers Sal and Vishal managed to capture Luvhari by using deadly *Shaktivaan* and carried him to Ayodhya. Seeing the intruder caught and brought to him, King Ram ordered a punishment of seven hundred lashes and then sprinkling of salt water on the wounds of the perpetrator. When Luvhariwas beaten with seven hundred lashes, blood oozed from his entire body and in some parts, the flesh had also come out. It was a horrendous scene. But no one there dared to ask Lord Ram to show pity. Seven hundred women were told to bring a pitcher full of Saryu water each which would be first mixed with seven hundred *sers* of salt and then the salt water would be sprinkled on the body of Luvhari.

In the meantime, Kushahariawoke and did not find his brother there. He found a heap of lotus flowers nearby, a snake lying there whose mouth was tied and the lake ransacked. The snake gestured that if his mouth was opened, he might tell the whole story. Out of pity, Kushahari opened the mouth of the snake, who was the leader Bachharnag, The snake told Kushahari the entire episode of how Luvahari went into the lake, the killing of all the snakes by Garud and his clan, plucking of lotus flowers and finally the fight between Luvhari and the two brothers Sal and Vishal from Ayodhya, capture of Luvhari and his being taken to Ayodhya.

Kushahari was furious with rage. He quickly ran to his mother and asked her permission to go to Ayodhya and get his brother released. He also got hold of some iron ingots and pleaded with Vishwakarma to make sixty-five knives. Vishwakarma was initially reluctant but with continuous entreating from Kushahari he agreed to make the knives. Kushahari took the knives and returned to his mother to get the knives blessed. Sita told him, "Remember you shall not use the knives against Ram, Laxman, Bharat, Satrughna, Hanuman and the milkman Bhukhla. You must know who Bhukhla is. He had accompanied me from Janakpur as a part of the gift from my father King Janak to tend to the three hundred thousand cows gifted to me after marriage. He is my confidant. I had given him a special long stick of Truth with seven joints, each joint measuring seven hand measure. If you introduce yourself to him, he will test the veracity of your words. For this, he will ask you to break the stick into seven pieces in one attempt. Then again he will ask you to join all the seven pieces in a single attempt. To join the seven pieces, you will have to sanctify a small piece of the earth using the dung of a young she-calf, stand on that earth, remember my name and meditate for Truth. If you do that properly the pieces will join by themselves. If the pieces are joined properly, he will be assured that you are my son. He will be your guide in Ayodhya and will provide you with all the help. He will introduce you to each person."

Thus taking the blessings of his mother, Kushahari left for Ayodhya to save his brother. It was evening and he decided to spend the night on the river bank. In the morning he saw seven hundred women with pitchers coming towards the river. These were the same women who had been ordered to bring water for torturing Luvhari. As the women entered just knee-deep in the river and got ready to fill the pitchers, Kushahri aimed his powerful *Agnivaan* (the arrow laced with fire) towards the women and burnt all their clothes. They were now naked standing in the river. To save themselves from the embarrassment all of them ran and hid themselves in a sugarcane field close by. A little later an old woman came to fill water. Kushahari hurt her also with his arrow. She could not lift her pitcher any more. She began crying. Kushahari took pity on the old woman. He went to her and asked the reason for a big procession of seven hundred women having come to fill water at the same time. The old woman did not recognise Kushahari. In her innocence, she explained to him that it was on the orders of King Ram who had caught the intruder of Kamaldah Lake and had decided to punish him severely. The old woman also described what punishment had been already given to the person in the form of beating with seven hundred lashes so that his body bled from everywhere and the poor boy had been crying with pain. Kushahari understood the whole action. He became extremely angry. He wrote a letter in the name of King Ram, "Seven hundred tigers are hiding in the sugarcane field on the bank of river Saryu. If you do not come to hunt for them by this afternoon, I shall behead them all and carry their heads with me." He gave the letter to the old woman with express instructions to give only to King Ram and none else. He then helped her lift the pitcher. The old woman quickly departed, her urgency now being doubled because of the letter to be delivered to the King.

The old woman reached the court and went straight to the King. She described her ordeal of getting injured by an arrow from a stranger and also helped by him to lift her pitcher. She then handed over the letter given by the stranger to King Ram. Ram lost his cool after going through its contents. He immediately announced all the brave people of the city to assemble and travel to the bank of Saryu to hunt the tigers hiding in a sugarcane field. Ram himself also got ready, the elephants and the horses were readied and he rode an elephant to the field. He ordered Sal and Vishal to join him along with their armies on the field.

On reaching the designated location on the bank of Saryu, they decided to set one part of the sugarcane field on fire so that hiding tigers would come out and make easy prey. On seeing the approaching the fire the seven hundred naked women had to leave the field. They somehow covered their lower private part with one hand and the breasts with another hand and came out of the field. King Ram was stunned to find his subjects in such a shameful condition. The entire army attacked Kushahari. Realising that all alone he would be no match for the large army, Kushahari jumped into the river and swam across to the other side. The arrows thrown by King Ram's army landed on Kushahari's body by just lightly touching him without doing any physical harm. When the army had exhausted their ammunition, Kushahari began killing them using his powerful *Shaktivaan*. Then he began beheading them using his sixty-five knives. He succeeded in beheading Sal and Vishal as well. But as was expected the knives did not affect the body of King Ram himself.

King Ram was so rattled at the loss of warriors that he had to summon his younger brothers Laxman, Bharat and Shatrughna as well. They all arrived but could not find a way out to either kill or capture the young boy on the other side of the river who had caused such devastation. Ram then asked Laxman to go and fetch Hanuman from the forest where he had been banished.

When Laxman reached that forest, he could not recognise Hanuman, lean and thin, almost famished and dying without proper food, Hanuman was a skeleton of himself. Gone was the strong and brave body which had spread terror in Lanka before and during the war. Laxman himself could not get the courage to face Hanuman but he had to obey the orders. He began weeping. Finally, with some courage, he described the difficult situation they had landed in and Lord Ram desired to see him immediately. Hanuman was in no position to move by himself. So Laxman lifted Hanuman and brought him to the court premises. He was nursed well for a week with the best food and medicines. Finally, Hanuman became strong enough to attend to the duties assigned by King Ram.

King Ram told Hanuman to go and catch the young boy on the other side of the river. Hanuman first tried to use his mace but the object landed on Kushahari's body as if a flower had touched him. Whatever tricks Hanuman would employ, it would produce the opposite and soothing effect on Kushahari. Hanuman finally tried to swim across the river and to make peace with the boy, asked him who he was. When Kushahari told him that he was a son of Mother Sita and his elder brother had been taken into captivity by the king of Ayodhya, Hanuman came to realise the whole affair. He was overwhelmed with joy to meet the son of Mother Sita and tears began rolling out of his eyes. He took the boy in his arms and began caressing him. He devised a scheme to unite Kushahari with his father Lord Ram. He lay motionless as if he were dead. Kushahari mentioned to people standing on the other bank about the death of Hanuman. The news spread like wildfire throughout Ayodhya. When King Ram came to know, he was blind in rage. He ran to take revenge on Kushshari and began throwing deadly arrows at him. But to his utter surprise, those arrows never touched the body of Kushshari, instead, they turned into soft and fragrant flowers before landing on his body. Finally, Ram agreed to make peace and asked the boy about his introduction. Kushahari replied, "I am the son of Mother Sita. The King of Ayodhya captured my elder brother Luvhari and tortured him badly. He is dying. I will not take rest until and unless I destroy the entire kingdom of Ayodhya".

Hearing this, Ram was overwhelmed. He asked Laxman to go and quickly fetch Luvhari from the prison. When Luvhari arrived, he was fed *Amrit* and given the best treatment. Lord Ram took the two brothers in his arms, lifted them and caressed them. Hanuman was seeing all the dRam. He now rose and in his usual high pitch shouted the praise of Lord Ram. Everyone was happy at the union of the Father and the Sons.

King Ram then decided to go and bring Sita to the palace. He travelled to the forest accompanied by his two sons. From a distance, Sita saw them coming towards her. She had no wish to return to Ayodhya and to live with Ram again. She prayed to Mother Earth, "O Mother Earth, be my saviour. I request you to split here and now and allow me to bury myself inside." Mother Earth obliged with her prayers. A small portion of land there split enough that Sita went down and buried herself. Ram saw this happening and ran to save her but it was too late.

After he saw Sita burying herself in the Earth, he lost the will to live. He went to the bank of Saryu, and went to heaven, leaving his mortal body on the bank of the river. That marked the end of whatever little had remained of the epoch of Truth, Satyug, and then began Kaliyug, the epoch of Falsehood.

* * *

VI

Sati Bihula

[Sati Bihula is a heroine-centric folklore where a virtuous young girl of twelve years, who is blessed to live long with her husband, is married to a man, the eighth son of an erstwhile worshipper of Bishahara, the snake goddess and the daughter of Shiva and Parvati. The husband is killed by Bishahara. But the brave young girl, now temporarily widowed, takes his corpse to the kingdom of Indra in Heaven and finally succeeds in bringing him and all his elder brothers, who had been killed earlier by a snake bite, to life. In return, she becomes an ardent devotee of Bishahara and worships her every year. This is one of the very few female-centric tales circulating as a ballad in Mithila.]

Bishahara (also called Bishahari) was the eldest of the five daughters of Lord Shiva. She was born as a snake when Shiva and Parvati were playing in a pond. Lord Shiva had given a boon to her that on Earth she would be worshipped during the month of *Shravan* (July-August) and those who would worship her would not have to fear snakes. The other sisters of Bishahari were Jaya, Samli, Dev Kanya and Datli.

There was a temple of Bishahara in Kamrup-Kamakhya on the bank of the pond known as the 'six-ghat' pond (there being six bathing platforms or ghats constructed on its banks). Fourteen hundred water pots filled with water were offered to the deity there. Chandradhar (or Chandu or Chanua Dada) from Champanagar in

Mithila was the chief priest of that temple. He was devoted to Bishahara and would perform the *puja* dutifully with all the religious fervour. However, due to some misfortune, his seven married sons were killed one after the other by snake bite. He lost faith in the Goddess, broke all the pots and stopped performing the *puja*.

His eighth son, Bala Lakhindar or Balaram was now due to be married. Chandu hesitated, thinking this son would also be killed and he would have to look after eight widowed daughters-in-law. But his wife persuaded him to look for a bride who was fated to have a living husband always. Thus after much searching, a twelve-year-old bride, Bihula was located near Kamrup-Kamakhya. She got married to Balaram. To protect the bride and the groom on the first night of marriage, the nuptial chamber was constructed by Vishwakarma himself using all marble blocks and leaving absolutely no opening anywhere.

Bishahara was not to let it go unharmed. She had taken a vow to kill all the sons of Chandu when they got married. She went and tried to persuade the serpent king Bachharnag to help her in killing Balaram. Even though Bishahara tried several tricks to persuade the serpent king, he was not agreeing for the reason that Bala was his fast friend. (See Box for the original Maithili narration.) They had been born the same day and had become friends entering the river Ganga. (Friends vows taken while in the waters of Ganga are considered irrevocable and ever-lasting.) He would not mind getting killed but he would still protect his friend because he felt pity for the young bride Bihula of only twelve years. How will she spend her whole life as a widow?

But who can defy the fate written by God Almighty? Finally, the serpent king had to agree to Bishahara's request and he came to Balaram's house. Bishahara with all her sisters was guarding the place on all sides in the night. Bachharnag went around the walls and could not find any opening through which he could enter. He again began crying and reproaching Bishahara. He could not come to terms with the realization that as Bihula would weep here so would his wife also weep in Ushari Dih. He strongly felt that killing was not a solution to anything.

जाइ दिन जग मे हम अवतरलौं
उशरी डीह मे हम जनमलौं
चम्पानगर मे बाला जनमले
गंगा पैसि कए यार लगौलियै
से सुरता सब मन परि अइलै
अइ से हमरा मारि नेरा दे
अपन जीब लए हम मरि जाएब
यारक प्राण बचा कए रखबै

The day I came to this earth
In Ushari Dih was I born
Bala was born in Champanagar
We became friends entering the Ganga
All these events flash in front of me
You can as well kill and throw me
I shall not mind at all for my life
I must save the life of my friend

The serpent king Bachharnag made many entreaties with Bishahara that he should not be forced to kill his childhood friend Balaram but Bishahara was adamant. When the five sisters discovered that it would not be possible for the fat snake to enter the nuptial chamber as there was no opening, they brought river sand and began rubbing over the body of the serpent using *Kush* grass, in the process making him thinner and longer. With some effort finally, they succeeded in making the serpent almost as thin as a human hair and pushed him inside the chamber.

Once inside the chamber, Bachharnag tried his best to awaken Bihula to save his friend. He went and curled himself around the neck of Balaram. Then he tried to caress the nose-ring of Bihula and hissing to create enough disturbances for her to be awakened but to no avail. He wept near the ear of Bihula. He even went down, curled himself around the leg of the cot and shook it but Bihula was so deep in slumber that she would not respond at all. Finally resigned to fate, he bit his friend.

He went outside to inform Bishahara about the death of Balaram. Bishahara was very happy and all the five sisters left the house. The serpent king, however, did not leave the house, went inside again and stayed put under the cot.

Bihula got up late when Balaram had already died. She found her husband's body had turned cold but still she could not fathom what had happened. It fell upon the serpent king to tell her the whole story about the death of Balaram. Bihula then went out, called her maid who had accompanied her from her father's house and told her to inform her father-in-law Chandu. The maid went to tell Chandu the sad news but he would not pay any attention. On the contrary, he began abusing the maid. Then the serpent king himself went and told Chandu how his son had been killed. Chandu started behaving like an insane person; he threw stones at the serpent. By that time it was twilight and people in the village had woken up to move around and commence their daily business. They came to know of the death of the youngest son of Chandu. While expressing sympathy, they also abused him for unnecessarily hurting the serpent king. This led to commotion around the house.

In the meantime, in desperation Bihula, using her virtue, prayed Brahma and Vishnu. Suddenly her sari caught fire. She decided to burn herself in that fire and commit *Sati*. But the serpent king opposed her plan and advised her to seek God's blessing so that her husband would become alive. Bihula agreed and decided to take her husband's dead body to the capital of Indra in heaven. Now Bihula was confident that with the power of her prayers to Brahma, she could bring her husband back to life as she was destined to live the life of a virtuous woman along with her husband. Her fate did not permit the life of a widow.

Before proceeding to the capital of Indra, Bihula prayed to Mother Ganga. Disguised as an old woman Ganga appeared before her and promised help if asked for. Bihula did not tell her what boon she desired unless Mother Ganga agreed to make a firm promise, not to go back on her words. After some hesitation, Ganga made a firm promise to fulfil her wishes. Bihula requested her to come and flow through her husband's village Champanagar. She wanted to take the corpse to Indra's capital through the Ganga River. Although hesitating, Ganga was now bound by her promise. She accepted the proposal but decided to consult her other six sisters. She called Vaya, Kamla, Kareh, Balan, Koshi and Tilyuga (all are the names of rivers flowing through Mithila) for consultations. Ganga explained the proposal of Bihula to all of them. They felt sympathetic and agreed. Now Ganga had no option but to flow through Champanagar. With Kamla in front and followed by Kareh, Vaya, Balan, Tilyuga and Koshi, they quickly reached Magah. But that was not liked by Bihula. She opposed the direction of flow. Then Ganga took the lead and went to flow through Champanagar. The villagers of Champanagar were overjoyed to see Ganga flowing through their village, an unimaginable feat. All of them congratulated Bihula and wished her success in her journey to God Indra's capital in heaven.

The serpent king had been following Bihula all along. Now he took the lead to guide her through the journey. According to the prescription provided by the serpent king, a barge measuring nine hand measures long and six hand measures wide was constructed using banana stems. Three mounds of lime and three mounds of flour were loaded on the barge. Bihula sat with the corpse of her husband on the barge and as soon as she remembered Brahma, the barge instantly commenced its journey without any effort by anyone or requiring any rowing. The villagers were surprised beyond all measure. They waved their hands and saw her off with their best wishes. The serpent king followed the barge in water.

After some distance, the barge turned southward in the direction of river flow. On the way a ferryman named Jhimla saw the barge with a lone young woman. He was enamoured with the beauty of Bihula and with ill intentions tried to come in the way and hijack the barge in order to marry her. Bihula prayed to Brahma who sent Goddess Kali to her rescue. Jhimla was defeated in his fight with Goddess Kali and fled the scene. Thus overcoming the obstacles, soon Bihula reached Kamrup-Kamakhya, near her father's village. Bihula wanted to meet her parents. The barge came to the bank and stopped.

Bihula's mother Mandodary was taking rest on a cot outside their house on the bank of the river. She noticed Bihula on the barge. She sent her servant to find out what had happened to Bihula and where she was going. The servant brought her the news about the death of Balaram and Bihula's determination to go to Indra's capital in heaven to bring her husband back to life. Everyone in Kamrup-Kamakhya, who learnt about the death of Bihula's husband, became very sad. In the meantime, Bihula's father Gunjan also arrived there. He consoled Bihula that it was destined and destiny could not be reverted. He dissuaded her from proceeding on her journey to Indra's capital. But Bihula was determined. No argument could shake her faith in her virtue and the power of her prayers. She told her father that she was going to Indra's capital not only to bring back her own husband to life but also all the seven elder brothers of Balaram who had died of snake bite on the night of their marriage. She saluted her parents with reverence and left the shore.

The barge proceeded further. Soon it reached a river 'Jonkia' known for its long and fat leeches (Jonk). The barge was attacked by the leaches' army. The serpent king advised Bihula to unload the bags of lime into the water. As soon as the lime dissolved in river water, the leaches began vomiting blood. They left the barge and fled to save their lives. Bihula continued her journey unhindered. Next, she encountered a sea animal called Raghav. This was a peculiar creature whose mouth was always wide open, with the top lip pointing upward towards the sky and the bottom lip downward drowned in water. The creature was ready to swallow the entire barge. At this instant, the serpent king told Bihula to empty the flour bags into the water. The flour made water locally very sticky and the mouth of the sea creature got shut and stuck. Now he could not harm. Bihula's barge continued its long journey through the seven seas. Once in Rajghat, the vultures descended from the sky to take away the corpse of Balaram. Bihula was now scared. But again the serpent king came to her rescue. Vultures began fighting among themselves to take possession of the corpse. With his cleverness, he threatened the vultures. The result was that instead of eating the corpse, the vultures began protecting it by spreading their wings.

Bihula finally reached the kingdom of Lord Indra. That was the time when Indra was being worshipped by the sages. All the sixteen hundred fairies had begun dancing to the tune of *Mridangam*. From a distance, Bihula heard the sound of *Mridangam* and that set her into dancing moves. Everyone was astonished when the *Mridangam's* tunes suddenly changed to the tune of Bihula's dance. They realised something heavenly had arrived and found Bihula dancing and moving towards the court. The fairies of the kingdom were surprised to find Bihula. They knew she had been one of them and had gone to the mortal Earth to live the life of a human being. Everyone began asking Bihula the reason for her return.

Bihula then described how she was made a widow because of the curse of Bishahara and that she had brought the dead body of her husband along with her. Her very touching story moved everyone there including the sages. The gods also were moved by her narration. They knew Bihula to be a very religious, virtuous and truthful woman who had done penance for long years. It was very strange that she had lost her husband and become a widow. But they also discovered that her father-in-law Chandu had antagonised Bishahara and forced Bishahara to seek revenge.

The gods started searching for the five Bishahara sisters. But they could not trace them. Finally, Brahma disclosed that they were hiding under the heap of waste flowers thrown after the worship of Indra. All the sixteen hundred fairies went in search of them but the five sisters managed to slip out. However, Bishshara was spotted by Bihula herself and caught from behind. She began to tell her story and pray Bishahara, "I spent years in penance here. I never antagonised any god. I have always been virtuous and truthful. I danced in the court of Lord Indra to please him. I used to take a bath daily in the river Ganga. I also visited Kashi and Prayag to earn some virtue. I have been always kind to the poor and hungry. I worshipped Lord Shiva, Gauri, and Ganesh. I even offered prayers to Hanuman. For my husband's well-being, I especially did penance for Lord Brahma and he gave me boon also. But still, you killed my husband and made me a widow. Tell me what my fault was."

This account of Bihula's religious acts moved all the gods assembled there. Brahma was moved and so was Vishnu. They all suggested her to go back and ask her father-in-law to give up his angst against Bishahara and begin worshipping the five sisters as he had done in the past in that temple in Kamrup-Kamakhya. But Bihula put a condition: She would go back only if her husband, along with all his seven elder brothers, was brought to life. The gods agreed to this demand. Soon they assembled seven bodies from *Kush* grass and laid them alongside the dead body of Balaram. All the eight were covered by a sheet. Bihula took blessings from all the gods. Gauri and Ganesh sprayed Amrit (the nectar of immortality) on their bodies. Immediately all the eight brothers came to life and sat before the gods. Balaram got up and began praying to the gods individually taking their names one by one. All the sixteen hundred fairies, along with Bihula, promised to worship the Bishahara sisters.

Being elated by the promise of receiving *Puja* from Bihula, the five Bishahara sisters asked her to join in playing *Jhumar*. Bihula hesitatingly joined. However soon it turned out that Bishahara along with her sisters was losing the game. Bishahara accepted defeat and praised Bihula very much.

It was now time in the kingdom of Indra to see Bihula off to Earth along with her husband and his elder brothers. Some of the fairies present there started singing '*Samdaun*', the tragic song of separation sung at the time of departure of a married daughter to her husband's house. Some others began preparations for gifts of betel leaves and nuts while some others chatted with Bihula making her feel happy. Finally, Bihula departed from the kingdom of Indra on the ninth day. All the eight brothers followed Bihula on the route. All the gods assembled along the route and blessed them.

Soon they arrived at Rajghat where the barge was waiting. According to the protocol, first, the eight brothers boarded the barge in order of seniority, the last being Balaram. Then at the end, Bihula climbed the barge. It soon started sailing at good speed. There was no hindrance on the return journey as they had the gods' blessings. There was no trouble created by leeches or other sea animals. They arrived at Kamrup-Kamakhya where Bihula's parents had been waiting. All the people assembled there praised Bihula's virtuousness, courage and determination to bring to life all the eight dead brothers. They all blessed the eight brothers as well.

The barge left Kamrup-Kamakhya and set sail for Champanagar. There was a large commotion in Champanagar when the barge arrived there with eight sons of Chandu. Chandu himself ran to receive his daughter-in-law and all the sons. It was simply incredible how Bihula had managed to get back to life all the eight dead brothers. Everyone had words of praise for Bihula. She had become an instant hero of the people. The entire Champanagar was celebrating their arrival. Bihula's elder sisters-in-law were weeping in joy, having been reunited with their husbands whom they had never dreamt of seeing at all. It was like a festive occasion. Everyone started making preparations for worshipping Bishshara and her sisters at Bihula's request.

In comparison to Bihula's virtues and religiosity, Chandu thought his material wealth was insignificant. He left his family and material wealth and went to a jungle to become an ascetic.

* * *

VII
Naika Banijara

[Banijaras were trader-kings of yore, who roamed with big caravans for years together, buying and selling goods on their way. The goods were carried on hundreds of thousands of bullocks. A typical trading expedition consisted of twelve years. The folklore about Naika Banijara extends throughout Mithila and is found in many forms, all having the same central theme about the travails of Naika's wife Phuleswari during his long absence, but varying in minor details. An unusual feature of this lore is a calf 'Tilanga' of unmatched physique and with supernatural powers and a cow 'Kapila' almost matching the qualities of the legendary Kamdhenu.]

Naika was the young prince of a small kingdom called Kamalpur. He had gone on a trading expedition with his father and his childhood friend Uttam, son of his father's minister. His father had been killed during the expedition by one of the robber gangs. Naika had been married in his childhood as per the existing custom. The tradition was to have a bride-bringing ceremony, the so-called 'Dwiragaman', when both the bride and the groom had grown into adulthood. The custom of Dwiragaman ceremony, a few months to a few years after marriage, was prevalent in Mithila even till the last century.

Naika's sister Tileswary was a sadistic woman who had been dumped by her husband because he could not tolerate her. So, even though married for many years and even after spending some time in her in-laws' house, she had returned and used to live in her parent's house. During the absence of Naika and her father, she behaved as the sole ruler of the kingdom. She always carried a whip and derived pleasure in beating the servants and maids and keeping everyone afraid of her all the time.

When Naika returned, he received a number of complaints of Tileswary's tyranny. Several maids had been bedridden due to her severe beating. Naika himself nursed them and provided food and medicine. He had also become an expert gemologist, stargazer, astrologer and much more. During this time everyone expected him to go ahead with the custom of *Dwiragaman* and bring his wife as he was a full-grown adult now. A messenger was sent to his father-in-law's city of Champa and a date was fixed. But the date happened to be close to the date of departure of the next expedition, which Naika wanted to be within a month.

Naika went to Champa for the ceremony and saw his young wife for the first time. Her beauty had been enhanced manyfold as she had entered into womanhood. After seeing her, he began repenting for having fixed the date of commencement of the expedition. In the night Naika told his wife that he was feeling hungry and that she should arrange for something without going out of the premises or without waking up anyone. Phuleswary, however, was a good organizer and quickly managed enough provisions and even milk with the help of Kapila that she could prepare a special *Radha-Kheer* (a rice pudding with lots of dry fruits and spices) which, according to legend, had been prepared by Radha for Krishna in Madhavi-Nikunj. Naika found the dish extremely delicious and he was fascinated by the culinary expertise of his wife. The next morning the bride and the groom were given a very warm send-off with lots of riches and with the calf Tilanga and cow Kapila, both of which were very attached to Phuleswary. Phuleswary treated Tilanga almost like her brother and he also acted in various ways to protect her from any trouble.

As soon as the bride arrived at the palace at Kamalpur, her beauty hypnotized everyone. Within hours she had further surprised everyone with her soft talk, humility and pleasing manners in her behaviour towards all the seniors as well as maids and slaves of the inner part of the palace. Tileswary was particularly jealous of her because she found herself eclipsed and also as per custom the reigns of the state would now pass on to the young bride in the absence of her husband.

Before leaving for his expedition, Naika received a strange visitor, a king, who had come from a distant land and wanted to pawn himself and his family as slaves to Naika in return for money to save his starving country which had been in the grip of severe drought for several years in succession. Both Naika and Phuleswary were deeply moved by the dedication of the king towards his subjects. Naika decided to take his expedition through the king's country, do whatever was possible for the people there and then only proceed further.

He had hardly enjoyed the conjugal life for a few days when the appointed hour for his departure arrived. Preparations had been going on for several days to load the goods on bullocks under the able supervision of Uttam. With tears in her eyes, Phuleswari gave a traditional Banijara-style send-off to her husband. While leaving, Naika took out the sanctified amulet worn by him on his arm and put it on the arm of his wife, telling her that the amulet would protect her in difficult situations. The amulet had the strange quality that its size would expand or contract according to the size of the wearer's arm and none other than the wearer or a blood relation could take it out. In return, he asked his wife to part with the calf Tilanga for the expedition. Phulesawry was only too glad to allow Tilanga to be part of the caravan as she knew he would protect everyone there.

The caravan consisted of one hundred and twenty-five thousand bullocks for the goods, hundreds of quality hounds for the protection of the caravan, and a reasonable size of the military with arms, ammunition and other necessary items. In addition, there was a set of personal security guards surrounding Naika himself who now rode Tilanga.

The caravan halted for the first night some fourteen miles away. There was a huge tree near the tent of Naika. *Bidh-Bidhata*, the legendary birds representing God and the Goddess, were sitting on that tree in the night and discussing the fate of individuals. Naika overheard them discussing that whosoever mated with his wife that night within certain auspicious hours would get a brave son who would be long-lived and bring name and fame to the family.

Naika was anyway desperate to meet his wife. Her pitiable and inviting face was still fresh before his eyes. He called one of his confidants and told him to open all the bells of Tilanga and make it ready. The order was complied with. Naika rode Tilanga and proceeded quietly towards his palace. Tilanga sensed the haste and began running fast. As they had been only fourteen miles away, it did not take Naika much time to reach the palace. He quietly went into the inner quarters and tried to wake up his wife. She was wide awake anyway as she could hardly sleep, thinking all along about the long separation. However, she did not expect her husband at all. She became suspicious and feared the person might be some thief or a stranger coming to outrage her modesty, knowing that her husband was away. (See Box for the original Maithili narration.)

She asked the most confidential question to which only the two of them were privy. That was related to the food served in the middle of the night at Champa. Naika gave the correct reply and he was let in. He told his wife about the discussion between the birds on the tree which he had overheard. She was soon in his arms.

Naika left early and joined the camp before others were awake. In the morning there was a murmur in the palace about a strange visitor to the Queen's quarters and Tileswary seized upon the opportunity to attack the Queen's character. She summoned a lot of elderly ladies and asked the Queen to explain to her how a visitor could come to meet her in the dead of night when her husband had just left in the day. She pleaded for her chastity and even undertook, as per the Banijara family's traditions, the difficult test of holding a red-hot iron rod in her hand without injuring her. Even though the elders absolved her of any wrongdoing, Tileswary was not satisfied. She kept simmering.

चोरबा रौ काल्हिए हम रौ एलियै गौना कराइए एलिएइ ना
चोरबा रौ हमरो स्वामी तेजइ मोरङ बनिजरबा करै ना
तिरिया गै नहिए हम गै छिऐ चोर भल चंडलबा छिऐ ना
तिरिआ हमरे नाम छिअइ नैका साह धनिकबा छिऐ ना
चोरबा रौ कतबो मीठी रौ बोलिया बौलबें तूँ करबे ना
रामा रौ तब बोलइए नैका अब बनिजरबा बोलै ना

O Thief, I came here only yesterday after Dwiragaman
O Thief, my husband has left me for business at Morang
O Lady, I am neither a thief nor a Chandal
O Lady, my name is Naika Sahu, the rich trader
O Thief, I know you will speak in a sweet voice
O Ram, then spoke Naika, the Banjara

Naika reached the parched country whose king had gone to him to pawn himself for the well-being of his people. He opened his purse to dig ponds and wells and construct dams over the drying rivers. His arrival itself turned fortunate for the country in that it brought rain as well. Soon people were happy and well-fed.

There he met a Buddhist monk named Devpadma who was very experienced in gemology. He had vast knowledge about the availability of different gems in the upper reaches of the Himalayas. On his suggestion, Naika began the expedition to the Neel Sarovar, a lake in the Himalayas where sapphire pieces were strewn around the lake like sand particles on a sea beach. He took a small party of select persons and left others along with the bulk of the caravan with Uttam.

As months passed, Phuleswary's pregnancy became visible. Tileswary was getting more and more impatient to act and dislodge her sister-in-law from the palace. She again called the elderly ladies and humiliated Phuleswary in front of everyone accusing her of carrying an illegal baby in her womb. This time, even though some of the older ladies feebly protested, Tileswary announced that until and unless the matter was settled after the return of her brother from the trading expedition, the Queen could not remain in the palace as it brought disrepute to the Banijara family. She assigned the servants' quarters for Phuleswary and took the entire operation of the state into her own hands. Phuleswary had no one to look forward to, she did not want to go to her parents in that condition which might mean further disrepute to the family. She thus decided to move to the servants' quarters for the sake of her child. An old maid was her only companion and confidant there.

Phuleswary stopped eating solid cooked food. Kapila was always present to give her milk. In addition, she ate only wild fruits which the maids could collect without inviting the wrath of Tileswary. In spite of this, Tileswary kept plotting to harm Phuleswary. As the Queen had passed the chastity test, Tileswary was afraid that the pregnancy might be genuine, Naika himself might have returned in the night to consummate with his wife and then the child might resemble the father. If that happened, her plans would be shattered much before Naika returned. She knew that within their hearts, people adored the Queen (now deposed). This fear led her to plan the elimination of the child. She quietly sent her confidant maid to the state's executioner, Dampha Chandal, with a request to cut the newborn into pieces for a handsome reward. She also managed to convince the midwife to take away the child from the unconscious mother and hand it over to Dampha.

While Tileswary spread her net carefully to eliminate the child, Dampha had other plans. He did not want to harm the future king of Kamalpur. He sent words to the old maid of Phuleswary to meet him at a designated place on the night of the childbirth.

Somewhere on their way to Neel Sarovar, there were signals of various types which the monk Devpadma interpreted as that of a son having been born to Naika. Naika himself had a dream about the birth of a son. But different games were being played in the palace.

When Phuleswary delivered the child, she was conscious enough to look at the newborn's face and console herself that the face was truly like the father. She also wanted the child to be taken away to a safe place. She unfastened the amulet from her arm and placed that on the arm of the newborn, prayed for his safety and became unconscious. The midwife, as instructed by Tileswary, took the newborn to an undisclosed location. The old maid of the deposed Queen also came out and went in a different direction so as not to arouse any suspicion.

The baby was transferred in the dead of night from the midwife to Dampha. He then went to the designated Kali Temple and handed over the newborn to the old maid as had been arranged. The maid finally deposited him in the lap of a childless potter woman who took it as the gift of God. Surprisingly, the cow, Kapila, kept visiting the Potter family and gave just enough milk there for the consumption of the baby. The old maid kept visiting the family frequently and had befriended the child from the early days. She confided with the Queen about the safety of the child.

After a few years, Phuleswary began regaining her health and as the signs of childbirth faded, she shone like a gem. She became so beautiful that no one could ever say this was the woman who gave birth to a child a few years ago. This very thought brought another dread to Tileswary: What if the pregnancy was denied altogether by the deposed Queen to her husband? The child had been killed and there was no proof. Then whatever she had done to depose the Queen on the pretext of illegitimate pregnancy would automatically fall through and she would be accused of falsely appropriating the reigns of the state. The only solution Tileswary could think of was to get rid of that wretched woman once and for all. She again took the help of her confidant maid and arranged for the midnight abduction of Phuleswary, which was not difficult as she stayed in the servants' quarters with hardly any protection. The plan was carried out and the abducted woman was sold to one of the Kumbha

Dom's men who had been scouting in the locality looking for beautiful women for his master's slave trade. Phuleswary was given a new name Phulia by Kumbha's wife. That was the name by which she would introduce her to the prospective customers.

Phulia decided to protect her chastity as far as she could. She told Kumbha that she was on a long penance and would not touch any cooked food. Fortunately for her Kapila was always around. She led an austere life, wearing only a white sari and eating wild fruits and milk. She kept herself busy playing Veena the whole day.

Kumbha's caravan with thousands of slave women of all hues moved from place to place but nowhere could he manage to sell Phulia. She was too saintly to be an entertainer for any prince or a rich young man. Finally when Kumbha's caravan arrived in the kingdom of Drona Nagar on the bank of river Ganga, Phulia was spotted by Droneswary, the local queen while she was playing a particularly melancholy tune on her Veena. The Queen was overwhelmed by the music. She sent for the Dom and expressed her desire to take Phulia with her. Kumbha demanded three hundred thousand gold coins which were paid to him and the new slave entered the palace of Drona Nagar king.

The arrival of the new slave brought enormous luck to Queen Droneswary. She had been childless all along but suddenly she conceived and gave birth to a son at the appropriate time. She then hailed the new slave as an agent of good luck, made her a part of the inner quarter and began calling her Bhagwati (the Goddess). Phuleswary in her new incarnation was protected and she had managed to maintain her chastity. She evn began cooking for the king and the queen. The days passed into months and years.

When Naika was returning after the end of his expedition, his caravan was attacked by the same gang of robbers who had killed his father in the previous journey. But this time with the help of Tilanga, Naika managed to defeat the robbers and kill their leader. Towards the end of his journey, he came to the kingdom of Drona Nagar on the bank of river Ganga where his elder sister Tuleswary, the queen of Drona Nagar, lived.

Knowing that her younger brother was coming to meet her on the auspicious day of Bhratridwitiya, she was ecstatic and told Bhagawati to prepare the best dishes she could think of for her brother. When the guest entered the inner quarters and Phuleswary had a glance at him from within the kitchen, she immediately recognized her husband. To the surprise of all in the palace, Tilanga also entered and smelling something, went straight to the kitchen and began licking the feet of Phuleswary. No one in the palace could understand the reason. But Phuleswary had found her brother on that very auspicious day of Bhratridwitiya. She worshipped Tilanga in the same manner as was done by Queen Droneswary to her brother, the new guest.

Phuleswary had prepared the very same *Radha-Kheer* for Naika, the brother of Queen Droneswary. Naika tasted the kheer and wanted to know who had made that dish. Surely there was only one woman who knew the recipe. Bhagwati was weeping inconsolably in the kitchen knowing fully well that the guest was her husband but she could not meet him because of her slave status in the palace. But Droneswary intervened and brought her in front of Naika, only to show him the new cook. Naika recognized Phulesary instantly and told his elder sister that Bhagawati was in reality his wife Phuleswary. Droneswary was surprised to find that the slave Bhagwati was her younger sister-in-law, who had been in the palace without anyone's knowledge. Phuleswary narrated the entire twelve years of ordeals she faced at the hands of Tileswary.

Naika's last leg of the home-bound journey now began on a very happy note, having been united with his wife much in advance than earlier anticipated. On reaching Kamalpur, he rejected all the elaborate reception arrangements done for him and summoned the court judges to try Tileswary and her maid for the charges levelled by the Queen. After initially denying everything, finally, Tileswary gave up when her most confidant maid also confessed to the crime. Although the judges pronounced death sentences for both women, Phueswary intervened and got them a less severe punishment in the form of banishment from the kingdom to any other place. Thus she saved her honour also, lest the general public would have accused her of taking revenge on the sister-in-law.

The Potter family was called and told to hand over the child to his parents. The child had grown into an adolescent of eleven years by now. Initially, they showed some reluctance because of the long attachment to the child from birth till that time. They also proposed some tests to make sure that the king and the queen were the parents of the boy. The amulet, which the queen had fastened to the child's arm, was proof enough as it was known that no one other than the parents could take it out. While the potter couple themselves could not take out the amulet, the Queen easily pulled it out of the boy's arm.

Finally, the boy was united with his biological parents. The Potter family was given enough wealth in compensation and also free access to the palace to meet the boy whenever they desired.

* * *

VIII
Deena-Bhadari

[Among the farm labourer class of Musahars (the caste known for extreme poverty but honesty of work) of Mithila, the brothers Deena and Bhadari are worshipped as folk heroes, almost bordering the status of a God. In a Musahar Tola or Musahari (the cluster of houses belonging to Musahars) in any village one would find a Deena-Bhadari Sthan, having a raised square mud platform, about 3-5 ft square, on which two bamboo poles about 30 ft high are erected symbolizing Deena and Bhadari, the two brothers.

Legend has it that Sabri, the scheduled caste woman, who fed Ram and Laxman raw plums during their jungle-dwelling days, asked a boon from Lord Ram that in her next life she should bear two sons like them. The boon was granted. Sabri took birth as the mother of Deena and Bhadari in her next life. Nowadays the clay idols of Deena and Bhadari are also accompanied by their mother's idol, who is depicted much like Goddess Durga. The festivities, with various performers singing the ballads and dancing, are held at many places and run for months. These are generously supported by Government funds.

Scholars interpret the tale of Deena and Bhadari as the tale of class struggle between the landed gentry, represented by Kanak Singh Dhami, and the free-willed aboriginals represented by Deena and Bhadari, who did not want to become slaves of the landlords and wanted to retain their original hunting tradition as their main livelihood. Although many

*Aboriginals accepted the dominance of landlords and had begun
working for them, even without wages, Deena and Bhadari did not agree
even when offered a little extra wage because of their superior strengths.
Musahars even today are regarded as the last remaining aboriginal
tribe although they are now part of the mainstream society and labelled
under 'scheduled caste' in the Indian constitution.]*

Deena and Bhadari were two brothers born to Kalu Saday and
Nirso, a family of Musahars in the village Jogiya (in the present-day
Saptari district of Nepal Terai). Deena was the younger and Bhadari
the elder. Both of them possessed a strong body and were well-
versed in the arts of wrestling and other martial arts of the time.
Unlike most of the people of their caste, they did not like to work
in the field and spent most of their time hunting. That was their
prime source of livelihood. Most importantly, they detested forced
and unpaid labour practices usually employed by rich landlords.
Not only did they abstain from such unpaid work, but they tried to
dissuade others of their caste also from going to such free errands
for the landlord.

The village was ruled by Kanak Singh Dhami, a local landlord
who was cruel and cunning. He usually forced the farm labourers to
work in his field for free. Even though the workers resented it, they
did not have the guts to oppose it. One day some of them gathered
and asked the landlord, "Why don't you ask Deena and Bhadari to
work in your fields?"

Kanak Singh knew that Deena and Bhadari were very
independent-minded and would not agree to his demands. Even
then he went and asked them to work in his field. He even offered
higher wages to them, considering their superior strength and
ability. It is said that Deena and Bhadari carried spades weighing
some eighty mounds. The brothers replied, "We don't care for
working with a spade and a trowel. We would rather go hunting
and live on whatever wild fruits and roots we can gather in the
jungle. More importantly, we detest your habit of getting work done
without wages."

Kanak Singh did not want to take a fight with the brothers and he returned. This infuriated his sister Bachiya who was a well-known witch. She hated the Musahar brothers Deena and Bhadari and wanted to take revenge. She got a big pond dug up in the west of the village and planted lotus flowers in the water. However, she quietly set a pair of king cobras in its water. Outwardly the pond had beautiful lotus flowers blooming in it. No one could suspect anything. The snakes began biting the people who came to fetch water from that pond and even the cattle and other animals who went to drink water there. No one would remove the carcasses and soon the place was filled with foul rotting stench. Bachiya challenged Deena and Bhadari to go and take a bath in the pond.

गामक पच्छिम कोड़ौलनि एगो लव पोखरिया
ओही पोखरिया मे धमिऐन रोपलनि पुरइन
ओही जन पैसिहs हो दीनाराम धरतs तोरा पनियादराद
ओही जन पैसिहs हो भदरी धरतs तोरा पनियादराद
घुरमी सहतै गे धमिआइन तोरो हम सधबौ
कुशक डेफ सँ नथबौ गे धमिआइन तोहरो पनियादराद

Dug a new pond in the west of the village
In that pond the Dhamiyain planted lotus
Enter that pond O Deena, a king cobra will bite you
Enter that pond O Bhadari, a king cobra will bite you
We will take care and shall tame you also O Dhamiyain
We will tie the cobra with a *Kush* grass O Dhamiyain

Deena and Bhadari accepted the challenge, went to the pond and bailed out the entire water, all by themselves. When the pond became dry, they caught the snakes, tied them with the rope made of *Kush* grass and threw them away. The pond was cleaned and fresh water was filled up. Thus they succeeded in defeating Bachia's designs.

Bachia did not give up. She was determined to take revenge. She went to the temple of Baghesari, the family deity of Deena-Bhadari. There she lay prostrated and without food and water for seven days and nights, praying to the Goddess. Finally, fearing the death of a woman, the Goddess appeared before her and asked her what she wanted. Bachia replied, "First you promise that you shall fulfil my wishes then only I shall tell you the problem. Otherwise, I shall die here in your temple." The Goddess relented. Bachia then narrated her wishes, "I want Deena and Bhadari to be killed somehow. They are like two thorns in the ruling of my brother in this locality." Goddess Baghesari was shocked to hear such a proposal. She loved her devotees Deena and Bhadari and always showered her benevolence on them. They were true devotees who would never blink even if the Goddess asked them for their lives. How could she make any plan to get them killed? But she had made a promise to Bachia which was also irrevocable. She had no alternative. The Goddess assured Bachia that her wishes would be fulfilled.

After a few days, the Goddess appeared in the dream of Deena and Bhadari. She told them to go to the Kataiya Khap jungle for hunting as it was full of game like deer, boar, foxes, and similar other animals. The brothers were excited about the prospect of finding the good game in the jungle as promised by the Goddess herself. Their mother however became suspicious as the jungle was known to be very dangerous. She went and called her brother Bahuran to accompany the brothers to the jungle. But there was a problem – It was considered a bad omen for three people to travel together on any journey. Deena and Bhadari were adamant as they were guided by the words of Goddess Baghesari. Reluctantly Bahuran accompanied them. On their way, they encountered several instances of bad omen but Deena and Bhadari were not to be deterred from their goal.

When the trio reached Kataiya Khap jungle, they were disappointed at finding the area completely devoid of any game. After almost a full day's search, they were exhausted and frustrated when finally they saw a lame deer fawn walking in the distance. Bahuran climbed a tree while his two nephews ran towards the slowly walking fawn. As they approached the fawn, it turned into a tiger and attacked Deena and Bhadari. Being brave and strong, the two brothers quickly overpowered the tiger and broke its two hind thighs apart. But by a miracle, which was the handiwork of Goddess Baghesari, the tiger soon came back to life and attacked again. The fight continued for several days and nights. In the end, hungry and thirsty Deena and Bhadari were killed by the tiger.

Bahuran came down from the tree and ran to the village to inform the parents of Deena and Bhadari about the death. In the meantime, the souls of the dead brothers took the form of *pret* (phantoms) and went to a nearby village named Ekaunsi where one hundred and twenty-one Musahar families lived. None of them recognized Deena and Bhadari. The phantoms narrated the story of their death and the corpse lying beyond the jungle. They requested the villagers to perform the last rites of the dead. But the villagers did not care to do anything. Then the phantoms went to a cloth merchant and begged for the shroud. The merchant took pity and gave them the cloth. They then performed the funeral rites of their own corpses. Because of ignoring the request of Deena and Bhadari to perform the funeral rites, the Musahars of the Ekaunsi village suffered heavily. Realizing that their trouble was caused by Deena and Bhadari, they began worshipping the brothers like Gods to please their souls.

When Bahuran reached the Jogiya village alone, the parents of Deena and Bhadari saw something amiss. They soon realized that their brave sons had been killed. The wail of the two old people reverberated through the village and many came running to console them. However, being extremely poor, Kalu Saday could not perform the last rites of his dead sons.

Deena and Bhadari took the form of yogis and came to their village. No one recognized them. They went to their own house and met their parents, narrated the entire episode of how they were killed by a tiger. Kalu Saday and his wife Nirso became very happy to meet their reincarnated sons. But Deena and Bhadari did not want to stay in the house. They went looking for Bachia, whom they thought was the root cause of their death. They learnt that Bachia had run away to a distant land beyond the Koshi River. They found that river Koshi was swollen. It was difficult to cross the river. They became very angry and threatened Koshi that they would dry it up if it did not calm down to let them cross. Koshi was frightened and the current in the river suddenly reduced considerably. Deena and Bhadari crossed the river and went to catch the wicked woman Bachia who had caused their death. They killed Bachia in the end.

The supernatural powers of Deena and Bhadari had attracted the attention of two women of Dauri village, a betel leaf grower and another a blacksmith, respectively named Hiriya and Jiriya. These women wished to get married to the two brothers. They had been worshipping Goddess Durga for a long time to get their wishes fulfilled. By the grace of Goddess Durga, Deena and Bhadari came to know about the determination of Hiriya and Jiriya in their dreams. They called the two women to meet them on the bank of river Ganga. They married them in the presence of Ganga and took them home in palanquins.

On the way, they were stopped by a wrestler strongman named Gulami Jat. Both the brothers began to fight with Gulami. After a prolonged fight, Gulami Jat was finally defeated. He then became their disciple and accompanied them on their way to the village. Further on the way, they reached Konauli. Konauli was ruled by a villainous strongman Jorabar Singh. He did not allow any woman to cross the road from east to west or from north to south or in reverse directions without being forced to spend a night in his bed.

Jorabar Singh had set his sight on the palanquin carrying Hiriya and Jiriya. He stopped them on the way. Deena and Bhadari began fighting with Jorabar Singh. Jorabar Singh fought valiantly for many days. Finally with the help of Gulami Jat, Deena and Bhadari managed to kill Joarabar Singh. People in Konauli cheered Deena and Bhadari. Womenfolk in the entire locality became happy at the death of Jorabar Singh. They would now be able to freely move around from one part of the town to another without the fear of getting kidnapped.

Deena and Bhadari were still in *Pret-yoni* (phantom state). They wanted to be relieved of that state and get salvation (*Moksha*). That would be possible only with the *darshan* (direct sighting) of God, Lord Jagannath who resides at the temple in Puri. The two brothers travelled to Puri in order to get a *darshan* of Lord Jagannath but the local priests forbade them from entering the temple premises as they belonged to the low caste of *Musahars*. Deena and Bhadari stayed near the temple for seven days and nights without food and water. Still, they did not get a glimpse of the Lord. Dejected, they then tried to push the temple base with all their might. To the astonishment of all the priests and locals, the temple began cracking under the strong impact of Deena and Bhadari's push. Before anyone could figure out what happened, Lord Jagannath appeared in front of the devoted brothers. No one else there could see this rare event. Deena and Bhadari were happy that their wishes had been fulfilled and they would get *Moksha*.

Musahars all around Mithila identify the brothers as their own Gods and have been worshipping them with full devotion and sincerity.

* * *

IX

Beniram

[Beniram is worshipped in Mithila as the family deity of two castes – Barbers and Karoris. These people have great faith in Beniram and it is believed that by worshipping this God, not only can one become prosperous but also can ward off the threat caused by witches to children and cattle as well. He is worshipped every year on the first day after the new moon day in the month of Chaitra. His clay idol is imagined like Vishnu, with a flag in one hand, a light torch in another and a bow-and-arrow in the third. The fourth hand is raised as if he is blessing the devotee. He is seated on a tiger.

Scholars believe that Beniram might have been a brave person during the days of anarchy in Mithila who fought some attackers and defeated them. He earned the praise of the local population and later got the status of a cult figure. His fellow caste people began his worship. A lawyer of the barber caste has even composed Beniram Chalisa, a collection of forty couplets on the lines of the famous Hanuman Chalisa.]

A barber named Lekha Thakur lived in the kingdom of Parauli. He was a very religious person. Every day in the morning, he would worship the Sun God and other fifty-six crore gods before starting his daily business. His fame spread far and wide, both on the earth and in heaven.

Once, Lekha Thakur decided to seek the blessings of a celebrated Guru. He had heard that those who do not follow a Guru do not end the cycle of birth and rebirth and never attain salvation (*Moksha*). He decided to travel to the kingdom of Lord Indra in heaven.

As it was destined, he soon reached the kingdom of Indra without any difficulty. There, he met Vishwakarma. He prayed to Vishwakarma to make him his disciple. As Vishwakarma knew that Lekha Thakur was not an ordinary being but rather had divine connections, he did not think it proper to make such a person his disciple. But Lekha Thakur persisted, and in the end, Vishwakarma yielded. He admitted Lekha Thakur among the group of disciples and made him the storekeeper. Lekha Thakur became very happy to find a Guru at last. He began a new life serving the Guru and worshipping the gods.

Once, it was decided to organise a special Vishnu Yajna in the capital of Indra. A barber was needed to collect firewood for the Yajna. Several gods wanted Lekha Thakur to be commissioned for this act, but the Sun God objected because the barber was unmarried. It is customary to employ only married barbers for the success of the Yajna. It was decided that Lekha Thakur should get married soon. The task was assigned to the Sun God.

There lived a Karori (a nomadic tribe) named Hemanchan Raut in the village of Mayna-Mahpura. He had a daughter named Godhan. This girl was highly devoted to the gods. Because of her pious nature, she was also called Godhan Sati. She had made it her daily routine to worship Lord Shiva in addition to other gods. She would offer her prayers to the Sun God immediately after taking a bath, still in wet clothes. Seeing her devotion and her growing age, Hemanchan made private arrangements for her bathing by digging a well in the courtyard and covering it with curtains. Because of the demands of his trade, he would be travelling most of the time and would be away from home. He was very concerned about the chastity of his daughter. With a special chastity balance, he would weigh his daughter's chastity every day and would be satisfied if the weight was found to be less than that of a single hibiscus flower.

Time passed by. Godhan attained the age of marriage. Because her father would be away on business, she was worried that he was not paying sufficient attention to the job of finding a suitable groom for her. She took the initiative herself and prayed to Lord Shiva, "O Lord Shiva, I have been worshipping you since the time I started walking. But you don't take pity on me. Can't you find a suitable husband for me?" Listening to the prayers of his longtime devotee, Lord Shiva appeared before Godhan and asked her what she wanted. She put forth her demand: "I seek a fully devoted and religious husband who, like me, should also be devoted to God. At this age, I don't find anyone other than Lekha Thakur suitable to become my husband. He is currently a storekeeper for his Guru Vishwakarma in the kingdom of Lord Indra. I pray to you to arrange my marriage with him alone."

Lord Shiva was moved and decided to help her. He immediately transformed himself into a Yogi and reached the court of Vishwakarma. Even though in disguise, Vishwakarma recognised Lord Shiva and got alarmed. He wondered what made Lord Shiva travel all the way from his abode on Mount Kailas to his (Vishwakarma's) court. He politely saluted Shiva and asked him the reason for coming to his court. Shiva stressed that he would tell the purpose only if Vishwakarma took the irrevocable oath. Vishwakarma obliged by taking the designated oath in the form, "First promise, second promise, third promise; if I go back on my words, I should be sent to the deepest hell".

Having thus satisfied himself, Shiva asked Vishwakarma to arrange the marriage of his disciple Lekha Thakur with Godhan Sati. Vishwakarma knew that Lekha Thakur did not want to get married as he wished to live a peaceful life with the Guru. But now Vishwakarma was in a bind because of his promise to Shiva. He called Lekha Thakur and explained everything. Lekha Thakur agreed to the proposal to save the promises of his Guru. Shiva took Lekha Thakur along and departed for Mount Kailas.

On the way, Shiva explained to Lekha Thakur, "My devotee Godhan Sati will marry only you and none else. If you do not marry her, she will commit suicide. Then you will be accused of killing a woman, for which the penance is equivalent to that of killing seven cows. Hence, it is better that you accept the proposal of marriage." Lekha Thakur agreed and kept his three useful tools (the leather sharpener, knife, and mirror) carefully with him.

Godhan Sati, in the meantime, had been camping at the Shiva temple, weeping all along about her fate. Her weeping and wailing were so heart-wrenching that both heaven and earth began shaking. All the living beings pitied her. Just around that time Shiva appeared there with Lekha Thakur and told Godhan, "O Sati, here is the person whom you desired as your husband and for whom you have been weeping. Now get married to him so that your wishes are fulfilled."

Godhan Sati stared at Lekha Thakur for a while. Then to test his truthfulness, she threw several magic tantrums but Lekha Thakur was unaffected. Meanwhile, Lekha Thakur himself was contemplating, "How can I marry this girl, even though pious and a devotee of Lord Shiva, belonging to an inferior Karori caste than that of myself?" Just at that moment, Godhan played a different magic trick which rattled Lekha Thakur. This led to his knife jumping out of his bag and hitting straight the middle partition of Godhan's head, also called '*siunth*'. The knife's impression was just deep enough to cause some blood to flow and make a good red mark over her hair partition, just like a girl gets a vermillion mark on her *siunth* after her marriage. Lekha Thakur was stunned but he could not backtrack. The marriage was thus solemnized without his consent or action.

Lekha Thakur took Godhan Sati to his ancestral village home. Godhan found out that there was a sandalwood tree in their courtyard. A peacock and a cuckoo sat on the tree and used to talk between them. Her in-laws were blind and addicted to hookah. She used to begin her daily routine in the usual way, nursing her in-laws, caring for her husband and taking care of the household. In due course she became pregnant.

After some time Lekha Thakur got an invite from the two witches, Jasia and Basia, of the kingdom of Morang (present-day Nepal, the town of Viratnagar and adjoining areas). They wanted to take Lekha Thakur in their possession by the tricks of witchcraft. Lekha Thakur kept walking for seven days and seven nights and then he reached Morang. The two witches, Jasia and Basia, applied themselves with the traditional sixteen forms of makeup, decorated their bodies with thirty-two varieties of ornaments, wore the finest silk dresses and appeared in front of Lekha Thakur to charm him. Whatever the tricks of witchcraft the two women threw on Lekha Thakur, he successfully neutralized them by chanting the name of his Guru and symbolically cutting the trap with his knife. But for once he forgot to utter the name of his Guru. Just at that instant Jasia and Basia threw a *sikia* arrow at him. This rattled Lekha Thakur. He got converted into a parrot. The two women quickly imprisoned the parrot in a cage and put the cage in a deep well. The well was then covered with a stone piece weighing eighty *maunds*. Over the stone piece, they planted special bamboo saplings which would grow very fast. Thus Lekha Thakur was imprisoned completely incognito.

In his ancestral village, his pregnant wife Godhan Sati was subjected to ridicule and mockery by the womenfolk of neighbouring households. One day even her mother-in-law began to accuse her of infidelity. But she kept her cool and spent time with utmost caution and patience.

She gave birth to a male child at the end of the pregnancy period. The child showed unnatural characteristics and began to ask questions to his mother just after birth, to the surprise of all. People whispered that he was endowed with divine components. The child was very curious about his father but poor Godhan was not able to tell him anything about his father with certainty. She only vaguely knew that he was in the captivity of the witches in Morang which she did not want to reveal. The baby jumped out of the mother's lap and started demanding – "I shall not sit in your lap, neither shall I drink your milk until you tell me the whereabouts of my father."

Godhan was frightened by the baby's tantrums. She was not able to understand whether the child was human, or some ghost or other wandering soul who wanted to know the whereabouts of his father. She did not want to lose the child. She thought that if she told him anything related to the captivity of her husband, the boy might as well run away from her and go in search of his father. Who knows the young child might also land in the same trap which befell the father.

गोदिओ ने खेलबौ गे मैया
दूधो नहि पीबौ
जल्दी बता दे पिता के उदेस

I shall not play in your lap
Neither shall I drink milk
Tell me quickly the whereabouts of my father

Sati Godhan summoned her family priest Kare Pandit to learn about the child's future. She sent her servant Jhimna to call the Pandit with all due respect and attention. Kare Pandit had been readying his books on astrology immediately after hearing the news of the birth of the son of Lekha Thakur. He expected good income in the form of donations and honorary wages. He departed for the house of Lekha Thakur with Jhimna. He examined the palm of the child, and his forehead and made some calculations based on the book's formulae. He then proclaimed to Godhan, "This child is no ordinary child. He is an incarnation of God. He should be called Beniram. He will be famous as a brave person who will always protect the common people, destroy evil and be kind to all. There is nothing to be afraid of. Because he has divine elements, he shows unusual characteristics."

The priest's predictions made Godhan happy. She measured a square piece of the earth having a length of one and a quarter hand measure, spread a black blanket over it, seated Kare Pandit over the blanket and with all due respect offered him a hefty sum as present for the wellbeing of Beniram. The priest went back happily.

The boy Beniram continued with his tantrums. He was all the time inquiring about his father. Finally, Godhan yielded and told him about the captivity of his father by witches Jasia and Basia of Morang.

Beniram was extremely annoyed at the news of his father's captivity. He decided to go to Morang and get his father released from the clutches of those wicked witches. He took his friend, Jhataha Pandit, son of Kare Pandit, along with him and the two commenced the journey to Morang.

Godhan arranged for a special horse for them for the journey. The horse, named Hansraj, was also very special, being born to specially serve Beniram. But without any master to handle him, he had become sick. Godhan Sati tended to Hansraj and within a few days, he regained his strength. With the mother's tender feelings, Godhan wished her son on the journey and sent him off with the blessings, "Your body should become stone-hard, which would neither be cut with any weapon nor it can be destroyed in any manner". As soon as Beniram rode with his friend Jhataha Pandit, the horse began taking to the skies as if wings had been attached to him.

In no time the two friends reached the boundary of the kingdom of Morang and landed in a thick forest. Beniram tied the horse to a sandalwood tree in the jungle and both the friends began taking a little rest under the same tree. They heard the roars of wild animals. Jhataha Pandit was afraid; he quickly climbed to the sandalwood tree. Beniram on the other hand went into meditation praying Niranjan God.

The forest was inhabited by seven hundred tigers and tigresses belonging to Jasia and Basia. Their job was to guard the forest from intruders. They had not seen intruders for a long time. So they were very happy when Beniram entered the forest with his friend and his horse. The tigers also were confused as to who should attack whom. In any case, the feed was too little for their large population. They started quarrelling. In the confusion, Beniram got a chance. He took each tiger and holding its tail would throw it to such a long distance that the animal would not survive. When he had killed almost the entire population, a lame tigress and a one-eyed tiger somehow managed to escape and run to Jasia and Basia to tell the story of the arrival of someone who had killed the entire tiger population of the forest.

The women were alarmed. They took fourteen hundred sachets of a special magic powder made using witchcraft and hid in their pigtails, another fourteen hundred sachets in their saris, some hidden under the eyelashes, some under their teeth and they arrived in the jungle where Beniram was sitting under meditation. They began raining the powders from the sachets. A normal human being would have quickly fainted but Beniram was unaffected. After several attempts at various tricks of witchcraft, they managed to disturb the concentration of Beniram. That was when he was affected also. The women quickly turned him into a stone statue. All-round gloom set over the entire world. An outpouring of grief emanated from every corner including those from heaven.

Godhan Sati came to know of the fate of her son quickly through her meditation. She began crying, even gods could not console her. However, the outcry resulted in Beniram being liberated from the stone statue. He attacked the two women, Jasia and Basia, and killed them after disarming them of their sorcery powers through his meditative powers. People in Morang heaved a sigh of relief at the death of the dreaded witches.

Beniram then went to the place where clusters of special bamboo were growing. He cut all the bamboo, dug all the roots and then he could see the large stone piece under which his father was kept under captivity in the form of a parrot. He managed to lift the stone slab and take hold of the parrot. He turned the parrot into a human being and the father and son were united. Lekha Thakur wept at seeing his brave son. He was very happy now.

The two returned to their village in the kingdom of Parauli and began living a simple life as a barber family.

Soon there was an important event in a nearby village where a rich oilman wanted to celebrate the birth hair shaving ceremony of his grandson with great pomp. For this, he had wished for some *Bhagat* (a sorcerer who gets possessed by spirits, good or evil, and acts to treat people's ailments and psychological disorders while under possession) to come and worship the family deity and the Sun God. Several famous *Bhagats* of the kingdom had been called to perform the *puja*. But they all were attacked by the magic of a witch named Mohari and succumbed to her tricks, having been taken into captivity. The oilman was very worried at this turn of events. Beniram came to know of such a problem and went to help the oilman without any invitation. He first neutralized the magic tantrums of Mohri, got all the *Bhagats* freed and then performed the *puja* himself. There was all round applause for Beniram. The hair-shaving ceremony of the child was held in an atmosphere of happiness and gaiety, free from any disturbance. Beniram became famous as a successful *Bhagat* as well. He would then receive frequent invitations wherever there was to be a *puja* of the Sun God.

Once some dacoits attacked the kingdom of Parauli and killed thousands of cows. There was an outcry at this ghastly incident. When Beniram came to know of the killing of cows, he went there, chanted some mantras with the water of the river Ganga in his hand and then sprinkled that water on the corpses. All the cattle came alive. Since that time, Beniram was called by people whose cattle became sick or had some other problems.

Once, Beniram encountered a woman on the road who was weeping inconsolably. On being questioned, she told Beniram that she was childless and was being mistreated by her in-laws in many ways resulting in her leading a very miserable life. Beniram consoled her and blessed her that she would bear a child. His blessings worked miracles for the woman who soon became pregnant and gave birth to a male child. Since then her family began worshipping Beniram.

Likewise, Beniram became known for his magical healing powers in almost all of society.

After a few years, the king of Parauli sent Beniram as a messenger to his daughter-in-law's village. This job was routinely done by the barbers. Beniram commenced his journey. He came across a jungle where the lame tigress and the one-eyed tiger, belonging to Jasia and Basia lived. They found a suitable opportunity and killed Beniram. The news reached Godhan Sati and she began wailing. His body was brought by the barbers of neighbouring villages and cremated with full honour.

Beniram became a folk legend and even today is worshipped by the barbers and karoris of Mithila. People believe that worshipping Beniram brings all-round welfare to the families.

* * *

X

Ganinath-Govind

[The sub-castes Teli, Suri, Kalbar and more importantly Halwai (confectioner/sweetmeat-maker) worship the folk-deity Ganinath-Govind. The tale of Ganinath belongs to Raj Palbaiya, which falls under the Mahnar police station of the present-day Vaishali district in Bihar. A temple exists even today on the bank of river Ganga, some eight kilometres from Mahnar town, where a big fair is held during the month of Bhadra (August) on the Saturday after Janmashtami (birthday of Lord Krishna). The confectioner caste is known to commence all important works on a Saturday only and they invariably worship Ganinath during that occasion. The tradition is to offer everything white to this folk deity.]

Ganinath was the father of Govinda. Legend has it that the gods Brahma, Vishnu and Mahesh once discussed that it was necessary to have some great personality on Earth who could control the evil systems growing in Kaliyug. They performed a yajna. A huge fire was lit using seven mounds of til (sesame), seven mounds of jau (barley), seven mounds of incense powders, seven mounds of Ghee, and other essentials. Out of that fire came a twelve-year-old adolescent. This person, born without parental wedlock, became famous as Ganinath. In the beginning, he was appointed as a cook for the gods in heaven.

The earlier cook, a Brahman, became jealous of this new appointee who could cook much better and tastier food. He plotted to remove Ganinath from that job. The gods came to know the plan and sent Ganinath to Earth.

Ganinath landed on a small islet in the river Ganga. The islet had elephant grass growing over a very large field. Ganinath found that an old man, a parcher by trade, was cutting the grass with a sickle. Ganinath helped him and soon the entire field was empty. He then made one single huge bundle of that grass and lifted it on the head of the old man. Surprisingly the old man did not feel any weight on his head, the bundle being a few inches above his head, as if floating in air. He could easily carry the bundle. Ganinath accompanied him to his village.

The huge bundle on the head of the old man drew the attention of the villagers. They were surprised and asked many questions to the old man. But the old man gave no reply and kept walking. When he reached his house, his wife, the parcher-woman, was weeping as there was no grain the in house and no one from the village had come to get anything parched during the day.

The old man dumped the huge bundle of elephant grass in a corner of the courtyard. Lo and behold! There came out a little girl from the middle of the bundle. The couple had no child. They were very happy to see the girl and the parcher-woman quickly embraced the little girl and adopted her, calling her by the name Khanesari.

More miracles from Ganinath were to follow. Ganinath felt hungry but the hosts were unable to feed him. They did not have a single grain of rice in their house. The woman felt very embarrassed. Ganinath sensed their embarrassment and asked the woman to look into the earthen pot hanging from the ceiling. There were just four old grains of rice attached to the outer wall of the pot. Ganinath asked her to take those four grains and cook the '*payash*' (sweet porridge). But there was no milk either. So Ganinath asked the old man to bring the she-calf, purify a piece of earth, keep the calf on the purified earth and start milking. Though hesitant, the old man obeyed. To his surprise milk started oozing out of the small undeveloped tits of the calf. After enough milk was obtained, the calf left the place all by herself. But there was another problem. For an unknown guest, the old woman did not want to cook in their old earthen pot. She asked her husband to go and fetch a new pot from the house of the village potter. The potter-woman however refused to give a new pot to the poor parcher without cash payment. No sooner had the old man turned back to leave the place than all the earthen pots getting dried in the oven were broken and the oven itself came crashing. The potter-woman became very frightened. She immediately called the old man back and gave her one of the pots. A miracle happened once again and the oven with all the pots became intact.

The parcher-woman cooked the *payash* in the new earthen pot and began serving to Ganinath. Ganinath, however, would not eat alone. He asked the old couple to join. To their surprise even after all three had eaten to their satisfaction, the pot was still full. Ganinath then asked the old man to invite the entire village. Very hesitatingly the old man went around and invited all the villagers to a feast of *payash*. All the villagers came and ate to their satisfaction *payash* served from the same pot. Still, the pot was not empty. Finally, on the advice of Ganinath, the pot was abandoned at a remote place outside the village. Legend has it that on that very occasion Ganinath had allotted the 'mool' (a root or a family-tree system for the origin of different branches) among the Halwai (sweetmeat maker) caste population of Mithila, which is being followed to this day for the settlement of marriages.

Time passed by and the fame of the unnatural and divine powers of Ganinath spread to larger and larger areas. He was now referred to as a Sanyasi (ascetic). Once, the only son of a rich trader (*Teli*), Tunki Sahu, died suddenly. On the way to the cremation ground, someone told him to approach Ganinath. He took the dead body to Ganinath and placing it on his feet, pleaded for divine cure. Ganinath meditated and soon the boy came to life. The rich trader then constructed a temple for Ganinath on the northern bank of the river Ganga. The entire population of the trading community

(*Suri, Teli, Kalbar*) and Halwais began worshipping Ganinath in that temple, which continues to this day.

When Khanesari became of marriageable age, the old parcher requested Ganinath to marry her. He agreed. Even after many years in wedlock, Khanesari did not bear a child. She was all the time anxious about not having someone to carry the family name. She became old. Once during Kartik Purnima (full moon day in the month of Kartik, November), she went to bathe in the river Ganga. On the previous night, she had a dream in which Sun God appeared and told her, "Go take a bath in the river Ganga and pray to Mother Ganga to solve your problem."

When she went to the river, she found that the river was in turbulence and high waves were appearing and disappearing. The fellow bathers warned Khanesari not to venture into the river. But she had the words of the Sun God in the dream. She went ahead. Pitying her, Mother Ganga appeared in front of her in the form of an old woman and asked her why she had decided to take a bath even though the river was in such turbulence. Khanesari explained the reasons to the old woman. She then told her to take a dip and spread her sari's corners. Whatever came into that corner, be it sand or water or mud, she should consume as a *prasad* (offering). She would get a son who would have elements of divinity and would be a saviour of mankind. He would be called Govind. She did as advised and some sand did fall into the corner of her sari. She ate that sand and returned happily.

Soon she became pregnant. When the time came for the birth of the child, a maid was sent to call the village midwife Champa who herself had grown old. The old woman presented many tantrums, saying, "After such a long delay Khanesari is going to have a child. Her husband is a person possessing so many miraculous powers. I shall not go to attend to her until and unless I am allowed new silk finery, make all the sixteen varieties of makeup and wear all the thirty-two ornaments. I shall go on a palanquin covered with red curtain and carried by four bearers." This led to the delay in her arrival for the delivery of the child.

During this delay child Govind in his mother's womb thought, "Why should I wait for this old midwife who is throwing so many tantrums? If she kept poor people waiting like this, half of the expectant mothers would die in pain and many babies would be stillborn. This woman must be taught a lesson."

While still halfway from her house, the midwife found that suddenly she got ejected from the palanquin and fell on the ground. All her makeup was smeared and the ornaments were also broken. One of her legs also was fractured. Still, somehow she managed to reach the house of Khanesari. By that time the baby was born and he was talking to his mother. He told her, "O Mother, don't let the wicked midwife touch me, otherwise I shall not consume your milk." The conversation was overheard by Champa who exclaimed, "O my God, from a girl I became an old woman, never heard such a case of a newborn talking to the mother!" She felt she had nothing to do, so she returned immediately. As she had developed bad feelings towards the newborn, she turned blind on the way. She realised her mistake, came back and asked the child Govind for forgiveness. Govind took pity on her and gave the eyes of a vulture. She could now see up to several miles away.

When the family priest was called to decipher the fate of the newborn, he had already heard about the divine elements the child possessed. Still, to confuse people, he told Ganinath, "This boy will be a demon if allowed to grow up. He should be killed immediately by burying him alive in a deep pit. Labourers were called to dig a pit but to their surprise, all their spades broke on the very first attempt of digging the earth. Then the priest suggested enclosing the child in a wooden box and throwing the box in the river Ganga.

There was a sandalwood tree in the courtyard of the house. Again workmen tried to cut the tree to make the wooden chest. But their axes would break and the tree would not get damaged at all. Govind, then himself began cutting the tree. The tree yielded. Govind, again himself made a suitable chest, sat inside and asked people to close that on the top. When that was done, the chest was taken to the river and thrown into it.

Mother Ganga herself came to the rescue of the child. The chest itself became a safe haven for Govind. People also by now knew that it was not easy to harm Govind. The priest admitted that he had spoken ill of the child out of jealousy.

While floating in the river Govind remembered his friend Karikh with whom he had established friendship while still in his mother's womb. He wanted to meet his friend. He came out and inquired about Karikh, only to be told that Karikh was under the captivity of notorious witches Nayna-Mayna at Kamrup-Kamakhya. He decided to set out for Kamakhya to liberate his friend. He sought his Mother's permission. Knowing the power of Nayna-Mayna, Khanesari was terrified at the prospect of his son going there. She was sure he would also be made captive like all others. But Govind insisted. Finally, his mother blessed him, "You will not be killed by anyone, nor burnt by anyone, your body will become stone hard." With these blessings, Govind commenced his journey.

His first stop was Morang. There he sought the hospitality of Kusma Malin. Kusma started dilly-dallying. Govind became angry. The effect was disastrous. Kusma's mother-in-law became blind. Govind left her place. Kusma came running after him and prayed to him, "Forgive me, Govind, I became arrogant and failed to recognise you." But Govind did not listen to her.

He then went to the house of a Domin (a caste very low in the social hierarchy, engaged in bamboo craft). Domin welcomed him and offered him whatever little she had. Govind was very pleased. He blessed her, "From now onwards, no auspicious event in any family in the society will be completed without taking bamboo baskets." This tradition persists in the rural society of Mithila.

The next day Govind was already in Kamrup-Kamakhya. The witches Nayna-Mayna came to know about his entry into their territory. Nayna sent three hundred young witches to destroy the newcomer. But when the young witches saw Govind, they could not believe their eyes. They had never seen such a handsome young man. They could not understand whether the body of the newcomer was made of gold by a goldsmith or it was chiselled out of some expensive sandalwood by a carpenter or made smooth by a potter.

All of them fell in love with him. But suddenly they recalled their mistress Nayna-Mayna's instructions. One of the young witches asked him, "Wherefrom have you come young man, who are your parents? Have you lost wealth in your house that you made such a dangerous journey?" Govind replied in the same tone, "I am coming from the kingdom of Palbaiya, my father is Ganinath and my mother is Khanesari Sati. Nothing has happened in my house, no loss of wealth or health. I have come to get my friend Karikh released from the captivity of Nayna-Mayna. That is my mission." He further added with a bit of sarcasm and pride "For others Kamakhya may be a den of witches but for me, it is like my in-law's place."

गरभ इयार हमर कारिख दुलरुआ
सेहो पड़ल नयना के बनिसार
कारिख गोहनिञा हम अएली गे जोगिनिञा
देखबै मे नयना-मयना सारि
सबके लेखे कामरु जादूके भंडरबा
हमरा लेखें ससुसारि

Karikh is my friend since we were in wombs
He is now in Nayna's captivity
I have come to get him released O witches
Nayna-Mayna is like my sisters-in-law
For others Kamru may be the den of witchcraft
For me it is the place of my in-laws

The young witches took this as an abuse to them and were very angry with Govind. Still, as they had developed a liking for the young man, one of them advised, "You do not realise the perils here young man. Your life is in great danger. Think that some of the witches may be planning to have you for breakfast while some others may prefer to eat you during lunch. We all entreat you to show good sense and return without bothering for your friend Karikh."

Govind laughed at this suggestion and repeated, "For others, Kamakhya may be a den of witches but for me, it is like my in-law's place. I repeat my resolve that I shall go only after getting my friend Karikh released from captivity."

The young witches changed their track. They now wanted to trap him. So one of them offered, "If you say that Kamakhya is your in-law's place, you must take a *pan-supari* (betel leaf and nut) from us, who are like your sisters-in-law. You must know this is a custom both here and in your Mithila."

Govind saw through the trap and replied, "My father is an ascetic and I am a Yogi. I have never tasted *pan-supari.*"

The witches then decided to capture the newcomer by throwing special powders which they had brought in pouches concealed in their dresses. Govind easily neutralised the effect of those powders. Then the witches threw *Agni-Baan* (arrows with fire burning at the tips). But when that fire touched Govind it produced the effect of a cool breeze. Not to be let down, the witches then threw arrows with cobras at the tips. Govind neutralised them by releasing arrows with eagles sitting on the tip. Finally, the witches were defeated.

When the news of the defeat of the witches reached Nayan-Mayna, the two planned another wider trap. In no time they set up a big witches market where the witches, dressed in their fineries with all the best makeup and decorative ornaments, sat along the road to seduce Govind. But all this did not affect Govind. Instead, Govind was now determined to catch the senior witches Nayna-Mayna. After several attempts at changing forms and trying to run away, the witches were finally caught by Govind.

When Govind asked them about the place where Karikh had been imprisoned, they refused to divulge the location. Then

Fekuram, a trusted lieutenant, who had been sent to assist Govind, began torturing the two women. Finally, they yielded and pointed to a location which had large cluster of bamboo growing.

Fekuram went there, cut all the bamboo, and then found a stone slab under which there was an eighty miles deep mine. Karikh was placed at the bottom of the mine, his eyes blindfolded, molten lead poured in his ears, all the twenty fingers were nailed to the ground, and an eighty-mound stone slab was placed on his chest. Karikh was finally freed and brought to the surface. Similarly, all other captives of the witches were also freed and sent to their respective places.

With his friend Karikh and the two witches Nayna-Mayna in their captivity, Govind commenced his journey back to the village of Karikh where his parents had been waiting for the return of their son. Karikh's mother Tiria Sati was overwhelmed to see her son after almost twelve years. She was surprised to see two women with them. Govind told her that they were the notorious witches Nayna-Mayna of Kamrup-Kamakhya. He wanted to kill the women but Karikh's mother advised against it as that would be treated as killing women and would bring a bad name to Govind in the world. Govind then neutralised all the witchcraft of the two women, leaving just two-and-half letters worth of knowledge which is mostly ineffective and forms the basis of all the witchcraft today. The witches were then released.

Govind thus destroyed the notorious witches of his time and earned praise from society. He, along with his father, is revered and worshipped by people, mostly *Halwais*, even today.

* * *

XI

Karikh Pajiyar

[The tale of Karikh relates to a cult which had been worshipping the Sun God. The ballad relating to Karish is usually sung over music played by mridangam, or beating of drums, sistrum and by clapping of hands. The countryside associated with the ballad is primarily Parauli, Sairadhar (in Nepal terai) and also some places in Saharsa and Samastipur districts of Bihar.]

Jotikh (a distorted form of the Sanskrit word Jyotish) Pajiyar was an ardent devotee of the Sun God, referred to as Deenanath. His little kingdom was in Parauli. It was his routine to take a bath in the morning, offer his prayers to Deenanath and then only begin his daily business.

One day Jotikh had an urgent work in the fields and he set out with a large contingent of ploughs and oxen to a nearby forest Keduli Van. He forgot about offering his daily prayers to Deenanath. As the day progressed, Deenanath himself became restless. Finally disguised as a poor Brahman, he arrived at his house and inquired about Jotikh from his mother Apura. The old lady told the poor Brahman that Jotikh had gone to Keduli Van to plough his fields. Deenanath followed there and found Jotikh so much engrossed in his work that he took no notice of the arrival of a Brahman there. Somehow Deenanath drew the attention of Jotikh and reminded him of his duty to offer prayers to Deenanath. Jotikh rudely replied,

"Today I had to change my daily routine. Now I shall take a bath and offer my prayers to Deenanath only after finishing the work in hand."

Jotikh could never think in his dreams that the poor Brahman in front of him was his very own adorable Sun God. But the Brahman was offended by the rude reply and cursed Jotikh. Instantly Jotikh lost all his property, oxen and ploughs and he became a leper. Before he could realise it, the Brahman had disappeared.

Jotikh was crestfallen. He came back home and asked permission from his mother and wife to allow him to go to *Keduli Van* for penance for twelve years. His mother Apura began to cry. Jotikh tried to console her telling that she would be taken care of by her daughter-in-law. But his wife Tiria Sati had special powers to foresee the future for up to twelve years. She immediately saw that now her husband would not return at all. She expressed her desire to accompany her husband to the forest. She entreated him, "See my dear husband, I am so new here, hardly a few days have passed before you brought me here after marriage. *Menhadi* (Henna or Myrtle) applied on my hands during marriage is still fresh; I have not even opened any of the ornaments worn during the event. I shall serve you in the forest and not disturb you in any way in your penance meditation."

But Jotikh would not agree. He advised her to go and spend time with her parents as they were well off and would not mind keeping Tiriya for a few years. Tiriya Sati was a very proud and virtuous woman devoted to only her husband. Anything else mattered little. She replied, "Let there be a fire in my parent's riches, I care a hoot for what my brother possesses. For me, you are all the riches and all my assets. Most importantly, I can bear any difficulty, tolerate any pain but not the pain of remaining childless."

Jotikh was in a bind. He was moved by the devotion of his wife, he knew she was right in all her entreaties. But he also knew he could not take her to the forest. Finally, Jotikh provided a solution to her, "I give you a flower. Keep this with you on your bed during the night. I shall visit you in dreams only. I hope your wishes will be fulfilled."

With this assurance from her husband, Tiriya Sati finally agreed to stay behind and also look after the old woman, her mother-in-law. Jotikh left for Keduli Van.

In due course of time, Tiriya Sati became pregnant. She gave birth to a strange child without any help from the village midwife. The child started talking to her immediately after coming out of the womb. The family priest looked at the palm, computed the star positions and came to the conclusion that the child was born with divine elements. He was named Karikh. People commenced singing, "Now that Karikh is born, this world will be a better place to live. Even the kingdom of Indra will be envious of the prosperous mortal world. Karikh will be the protector of all."

कारिख जनम भेल दुनियाँ आनन्द भेल
डोलि गेल इन्दर कविलास हो
सुरपुर डोलय कारिख नरपुर डोलय हो
डोलय लागल इन्दर कविलास हो

Karikh is born and the world rejoiced
The kingdom of Indra began shaking
The heaven is shaking and earth is shaking
Shaking also is the kingdom of Indra

Karikh's growth was rapid, like the phases of the moon. He was a brave and strong child from the early days. His tales of bravery became a legend among people. He feared none, not even wild beasts and poisonous snakes. He would catch a tiger by the neck and put a nosestring through its nostrils. He was an expert hunter. He would go swimming in all the rivers in his kingdom. There was a river Sayla where a pair of dreaded serpents, Nag and Nagin, lived.

No one dared to go for bathing in that river. When Karikh decided to go swimming in that river Sayla, everyone forbade him from going there. Not only did Karikh go to the river, but he also managed to catch the two serpents, tie their mouths with straw ropes and bring them to the villagers to behold. People were awe-struck at the belligerence of Karikh.

After a few years, Karikh asked his mother about the whereabouts of his father. She told him that he was serving a twelve-year penance in Keduli Van. He decided to go in search of his father. When Karikh left, his kingdom of Parauli looked deserted, which is described in the ballad in the following way, "Why is the town of Ayodhya looking deserted O friend, Why is the kingdom of Parauli? The town of Ayodhya is looking deserted because of the absence of Lord Ram O friend, and the kingdom of Parauli because of the absence of Karikh."

Karikh searched the entire Keduli Van but got no trace of his father. Then he went to Bhagat Mali to inquire if he knew anything. Mali welcomed Karikh in the traditional manner, washing his feet and making him comfortable with whatever he could think of. Karikh was not interested in those things; he straightway asked if Mali knew anything about his father. Mali took him towards the bank of river Ganga and pointed towards a *peepal* tree at some distance. He told Karikh that his father used to sit in meditation under that *peepal* tree.

Karikh left Mali's house and walked towards the pipal tree. But his father was not there. He could not find any sign of a human being around. He was now afraid that his father may have become prey to wild animals in the forest. He sat down there and began weeping. Mother Ganga took pity on Karikh and appeared as an old woman in front of him. Karikh touched her feet. The old woman asked him the reason for weeping. He described his fears about his father supposedly having been killed by some wild animal. Mother Ganga consoled him and told him that after completing the period of penance, Jotikh had gone to heaven quite some time ago.

Karikh wanted to meet his father at any cost. He took a journey to heaven and after some difficulties finally managed to reach there and find his father. He requested his father to go back to his kingdom in the mortal world. Jotikh Pajiyar however blessed Karikh and told him to go back and serve the people in Parauli. Karikh returned and then began a simple life in his kingdom.

Soon he learnt about the tyranny unleashed by the notorious witches Nayna-Mayna at Kamrup-Kamakhya. The duo had kept a large number of kings and others, including Gods, in their captivity by the power of their witchcraft. They enjoyed perpetrating terror among people as far as they could.

Karikh wanted to take revenge on the witches. He went to Kamrup-Kamakhya. Unfortunately, even though he possessed some divine qualities, he was no match for the varied tricks of those witches. He was caught and kept in captivity like others.

After many years, when his friend of the womb, Govind, went to Kamrup-Kamakhya and finally defeated Nayna-Mayna, Karikh was released from the captivity of the witches along with all others. He then returned to Parauli and ruled his kingdom as a benevolent and wise person.

Even today Karikh is worshipped by many families as their home deity because of his bravery, strong will to fight injustice and always seeking the welfare of common people.

* * *

Mithila : A Brief Introduction

History and Geography

In the Indian landscape, Mithila has been an ancient territory. Description of Mithila by various names like Videh, Teerbhukti (a distorted modern name being Tirhut) etc. appear in many old texts dating back to the Vedic period. Satpath Brahman and Brihdaranyak Upnishad are the main texts where even the geography of the territory is described as being bounded by the Himalayas on the north and by the rivers Gandak on the west, Koshi on the east and Ganga on the south. Of course, rivers have been changing their course and naturally, they do not provide a good reference point for the borders over a long period.

The most important description of Mithila is found in the Ramyana. Mithila is in the centre of this epic, being the birthplace of Sita. Janakpur, the capital of the Janak dynasty, is now in Nepal. Sita was born at Punaura near Sitamarhi (in Bihar). Mithila and its Janak kings are again prominently mentioned in the Mahabharata also.

Mithila is known to have 'philosopher kings' in contrast to the 'warrior kings' in other regions of the world. Being protected by the rivers, this land was safe and did not get influenced by foreign invasions for quite long. This comparative tranquillity led to the development of very high levels of intellectual activity in Mithila. This land produced some of the greatest scholars, philosophers and sages, consisting of persons of both sexes, contrary again to other world regions. King Seeradhvaj Janak, father of Sita, was one of the best-known philosopher kings. Yajnavalkya, Gautam, Kanad, Kapil, Kumarila, Mandan, Vachaspati, Udayan, Gangesh, Chandeshwar, Vardhaman and Vidyapati are some of the illustrious sons of the soil of Mithila. These are joined by Gargi, Maitreyi, and Bharti among the female scholars. Schools of philosophy like Purvamimansa,

Uttarmimansa (Vedanta), Nyaya, Vaishesika, and Sankhya were developed in Mithila. It was in Mithila that Yajurvedasamhita of the Vedas was composed which contains the celebrated Upnishad Ishavasyam – the foundation of the Vedanta philosophy.

After the fall of the Janak dynasty (the last king being Karal Janak), Mithila became a part of the Lichhavi Republic. This republic existed around the time of Gautam Budhha and Mahavir. Around 300 BC, this republic also disintegrated and the region became part of Magadh rulers. During the rule of the Maurya and Gupta dynasties, Mithila was also under the rule of those kings.

In the medieval period, Mithila is recorded as being a sovereign state ruled by the Karnat dynasty from around AD 1097 till AD 1323. Nanyadev was the first king and his capital was at Simarangarh (now in Nepal). This was the golden period in Mithila again after a gap of more than a millennium. Harisinghadev (accession to the throne circa AD 1307), the last king of this dynasty, is considered one of the most important social reformers in Mithila. After Muslim rulers of Delhi invaded Mithila, Harisinghadev is known to have fled to Nepal around AD 1323. He ruled Nepal also for some time.

After the decline of the Karnat dynasty, for about three decades there was anarchy, with local governors of Delhi sultanate ruling in pockets. Then Mithila was ruled by the kings of the Oyinvar dynasty from around AD 1356 till AD 1526. In this period Mithila's rule went into the hands of Delhi's Muslim rulers. Firoz Shah Tuglak appointed Pandit Kameshwar Thakur as the ruler of Mithila. The Oyinvar dynasty is proud to have kings like Kirti Singh, Bhav Singh, Dev Singh, and Shiv Singh. Shiv Singh is said to have revolted against the Delhi rule to have independent status for Mithila. This led to war. Shiv Singh's fate after the war is not known. It is well known that the poet Vidyapati was a contemporary of the famous king Shiv Singh. The rule of this dynasty is supposed to have extended from 1353 till 1526.

After this period Mithila was also disturbed under the influence of local Muslim governors. The whole region was divided into small zones ruled by local satraps. Later Akbar gave charge to Pandit

Mahesh Thakur, who started the Khandavala dynasty. This dynasty essentially ruled till the British period but with shrinking influence.

During the British rule in India, by a treaty held at Sugauli (presently in the East Champaran district of Bihar) in 1816, the British gave a part of the Mithila region to the Gorkha rulers of Nepal. Since that time Mithila has been divided, part in the bordering Terai region in Nepal and part in the state of Bihar in India. That is the reason for Janakpur and Simarangarh now being in Nepal.

A number of rivers flow through Mithila, prominent among them being Koshi, Kamla-Balan, Bagmati, Kareh, Budhi-Gandak and Mahananda. All these rivers originate in the Himalayas and have a large number of tributaries making the land fertile yet vulnerable to floods.

Map of Mithila

Mithila today is not a geographical entity but only a cultural region. There has been a demand for a separate Mithila state within India based on its linguistic identity but the demand has not yet been fulfilled. The Maithili language however has become part of the constitutionally recognized languages in India. In Nepal, it is the second official language. Social bonding between the two parts of Mithila (India and Nepal) is very strong, even today a large number of marriage relations exist and new relations are getting added every year. A map of the proposed state of Mithila in India along with the adjoining regions in Nepal is given here for illustration. For details on history, one can refer to [1-4].

Culture and Literature

Even though Mithila lost her political sovereignty in the 14th century, it retained intellectual supremacy for a long time. The intellectual pursuit of Sanskrit scholars consisted of Navya-Nyaya, Nibandha, juridical literature, dRams, lyrics etc. These were carried throughout India by the visiting scholars.

Karnat king Harisinghadev was a great social reformer. He started the classification of Maithil Brahmans and also a procedure for the registration of marriages. Detailed genealogy of Maithil Brahmans is available even today.

The world's first prose 'Varna Ratnakar' is supposed to have been written by Jyotirishwar in the 14th century who was a contemporary of Harisinghadev. During the reign of the Oyinvar dynasty, the famous poet Vidyapati was born. His contribution to Maithili literature is unparalleled. Maithili literature is a vibrant field even today and each year scholars are recognized for their contributions by the Sahitya Academy, which is an affiliate organization of the Government of India. In Nepal too, there are several such awards given through both Government and private agencies. A good account of the history of Maithili literature can be found in [5-6]. A recent useful book describing the social history of Mithila during 14th-16th centuries is by Yogkar Jha [7]. Some account can also be found in [8,9]

Mithila has been a seat of learning from old age and scholars from all around the country were coming here to learn and also for *Shastrarth* (academic discourse) to enrich their knowledge. Students from Bengal were particularly attracted to the Gurus in Mithila for their studies. It is the general belief that there were ten thousand students in the ashram of Pandit Bhavnath Mishra (popularly known as Ayachi Mishra) who was a great scholar and an exponent of Navya Nyaya.

The society in Mithila, as elsewhere in India, is divided into castes and sub-castes. The main economic activity is agriculture. An account of the economics of the region can be found in [10]. The social customs, festivals and rituals are all a byproduct of this agrarian lifestyle centred in villages. Very elaborate ceremonies are held for the child's birth, naming ceremony, *mundan* (shaving of birth hair), *upanayana* (sacred thread ceremony, for Brahmans), marriages, death etc. Marriage ceremony, in particular among the Brahmans and Kayasthas in Mithila, is not just a day's affair. Its various rituals continue for almost one full year both for the bride and the groom. A brief description of marriage rituals along with a translation of folk songs for various occasions can be found in [11]. Because of the abundance of ponds, lakes and rivers, people of all castes in Mithila, including Brahmans, have been traditionally fish eaters. Fish plays a central role in many folktales.

Festivals

People in Mithila celebrate various festivals with great fanfare. While many are celebrated at the community level, some others are celebrated only in individual homes. After the rainy season is over, one begins with Durga Puja in the month of Ashwin (a ten-day gala affair beginning on the day after the new moon till the tenth day), Diwali (on the new moon day in the month of Kartik), Govardhan Puja and Chitragupta Puja (next day after Diwali), Chhath (on the sixth and seventh day after Diwali), Makar Sankranti (on January

14th/15th) Saraswati Puja (also called Vasant Panchami, on the fifth day after the new moon in the month of Magh), Shivaratri (on the 14th day after the full moon in the month of Phalgun), Holi (on the full moon day in Phalgun), Ramnavami (on the ninth day after new moon in the month of Chaitra), Kark Sankranti and Juri Sheetal (14th and 15th April), Nag Panchami (on the fifth day after new moon in the month of Shrawan) and then Krishna Janmashtami (eighth day after full moon in the month of Bhadra). For newly married women the one-fortnight-long *Madhushravani* Puja in the month of Shravan is considered very important. Similarly, the *Kojagari Purnima* (the full moon day in the month of Ashwin) is an important event for newly married men when they receive handsome gifts from the bride's father.

People worship rivers as they worship the Sun, the Moon, the banyan tree, and the snakes. On certain auspicious occasions, like Kartik Purnima, Magh Purnima etc., people congregate at the river banks for a holy bath. Fairs are usually organized on such occasions on the river banks. One of the famous places for such a fair is Simariya near Barauni on the bank of River Ganga.

Women, being traditionally very religious, observe *vrat* (fasting) on the *Ekadashi*(the eleventh day after the new moon and full moon each month), several Sundays, all Mondays in the month of Shravan etc. and on several other occasions. In addition, married women specifically observe *vrat* (fasting) on various occasions, the most important being Vat Savitri (in the month of Jyestha) and Jimutvahan Vrat (in the month of Ashwin).

Art and Craft

Mithila has a very highly developed and rich folk art and craft culture. Madhubani paintings are famous for their minute details and combination of bright colours. Folk art from bamboo, straw and other reeds, cotton, wood etc. have been quite popular. Several authors have described them in detail in various publications. See [12].

Folk Tradition and Story-Telling

Mithila has had a long tradition of folklore, folk songs, ballads and storytelling. Since olden days stories have been woven around gods and goddesses, animals and birds, fairies, ogres and ogresses, *pretatma* (souls of dead people before liberation through the ritual of *Shraddha*), cursed princes and princesses, poor Brahmans and kings etc. A typical aspect of the Maithili folk story is the presence of a pair of god characters, *Bidh* (female) and *Bidhata* (male). The pair keeps travelling in the form of birds and usually takes rest during the night on some trees when someone in distress is located by *Bidh* under the tree. Generally, *Bidh* is very compassionate and prevails upon *Bidhata* to somehow help the person in distress. An account of the nature of folktales is given in [13,14]. Ballads have immortalized several heroes and heroines who were benevolent and brave and helped fight injustice against common people.

Further Reading

[1] Upendra Thakur, *History of Mithila*, Mithila Institute, Darbhanga, (1988).

[2] Radhakrishna Chaudhary, *Mithila in the Age of Vidyapati*, Varanasi, (1976).

[3] Stephen Henningham, *A Great Estate and Its Landlords in Colonial India, Darbhanga, 1860-1942*, Oxford University Press, Delhi, (1990).

[4] Jatashankar Jha, *History of Darbhanga Raj*, Journal of the Bihar Research Society, vol. XLVIII, Patna, (1962).

[5] Jayakant Mishra, *A history of Maithili literature*, Tirabhukti Publications, Allahabad, (1949).

[6] Radhakrishna Chaudhary, *A survey of Maithili literature*, Deoghar, (1976).

[7] Yogkar Jha, *Social history of Mithila from 14th to 16th Century*, Esamaad Prakashan, (2024).

[8] Ramnath Jha, *Vidyapati (Makers of Indian Literature Series)*, Sahitya Academy, New Delhi, (1972).

[9] Jayadeva Mishra, Chanda Jha *(Makers of Indian Literature Series)*, Sahitya Academy, New Delhi, (1981).

[10] Narendra Jha, *Mithila Rising*, Sasta Sahitya Mandal, New Delhi, (2014); Economy of Mithila : From Prosperity to Destruction (with special reference to Darbhanga Raj), Avanindra Kumar Jha, Lucky International (2024).

[11] Ram Dayal Rakesh, *Marriage Songs of Mithila*, Pilgrims Publishing, Varanasi, (2016).

[12] Upendra Thakur, *Madhubani Paintings*, New Delhi, (1982).

[13] Ram Dayal Rakesh, *Folktales from Mithila*, Nirala Publication, New Delhi (1996).

[14] Yogendra Pathak Viyogi, *Folktales of Mithila*, self-published, (2022); *Gonu Jha of Mithila (Tales of wit and humour)*, self-published, (2022); available online.

EXPLANATION OF SPECIAL WORDS

Explanation of terms related to customs and rituals prevalent in olden days in Mithila.

Gohari means taking away someone's troubles and solving problems of all kinds. It was usually carried out by persons in power or those having such means. It had several variations which included treating the ill and also curing people of the influence of ghosts etc. With tantric influence coming into the society later, this practice degenerated into a *Bhagat* system where the so-called *bhagat* claimed to be possessed by spirits, ghosts or even various forms of gods.

Anchara, is usually a piece of cloth tied to a sacred tree or a pole near a deity's place either in the house or in a temple as a reminder of an oath and also to have it fulfilled.

Gandharva Marriage: A form of love marriage sanctioned by society in olden times.

Dwiragaman: A ritual in Mithila, literally meaning second coming, where after the marriage of the boy and the girl as children or at a very young age, the husband would go a second time to his wife's place to ceremoniously bring her to his own house after both of them had attained adulthood. Now the practice is almost abolished as the marriage takes place among mature adults and the bride goes with the husband only after a few days of customary rituals.

Mound and Ser: Old units of weight, one Ser is two pounds, and a mound is 40 Sers. A mound is approximately equal to 37 kilograms.